DEAD
PRETTY

SAMANTHA TOWLE

ISBN-13: 9798652013424

ONE

He's here again.

That's the third day in a row.

He stands out to me because he doesn't look like the usual type of guy I see in here.

Okay, so the standard type of men who do come in the library, where I work, are typically sixty and over. And this guy is most definitely not sixty.

I would give him late twenties, early thirties.

He is also everything I would have been attracted to in my former life.

Tall. Built. Brown hair. Short on the sides, a mess of waves on top. Stubble. Eyes so blue that you can see the color clear across the room.

He unzips his well-worn black leather jacket as he walks inside, revealing a white T-shirt. Dark blue jeans on legs. Scuffed-up brown biker boots on his feet.

A messenger bag hangs from his shoulder. A motorcycle helmet in his hand.

I'm fairly sure he's new to town.

I would know if I had seen him around before. Not that I'm a social butterfly who gets to know people.

That was the old Audrey.

The new Audrey avoids all possible contact with people.

But I do pay attention, especially to people who are new in town.

The stranger runs his hand through his hair, messing it up more as he walks over to the table closest to the windows.

I watch as he rounds the table, pulls out the chair that puts his back to the windows, and sits down, giving him a view of the open library space, the reception desk, and the door he just walked in through.

But not the stacks that I'm standing behind, where I'm putting away returned books. Although, currently, I'm not doing anything but cataloguing this stranger's movements.

He sits at the same table, in the exact same chair, every day that he is here.

So, he's either a creature of habit. Or he wants a bird's-eye view of the library.

The old me would have faced the window and looked out at the view, ignoring what was happening behind me.

The new me would take the same seat that he has.

I know what my reason would be for sitting there. I don't know his.

And that bothers me.

Probably more than it should.

I didn't always used to analyze people like this. The old me would never have spared a single thought about why a person took a particular seat in the library.

The new me analyzes everything.

I can't afford to miss anything. I can't risk history repeating itself.

The stranger puts his helmet down on the floor beside the table. Takes off his jacket and hangs it on the back of the chair he's sitting on. Gets a laptop from his messenger bag, places it on the table, and opens it up.

He does the exact same routine every day.

And I watch him every day, like a creeper.

This guy could just be a creature of habit. And I'm acting like a total paranoid wack job.

The stranger's eyes suddenly flick up from his laptop and look straight at the bookshelves I'm standing behind. Like he knows that I'm here, observing him.

My breath catches, and I jump back, knocking into the shelves behind me.

"Shit," I hiss, rubbing my elbow that I just banged on the wood.

When the ache in my arm subsides, I take a measured step back to the shelves and peer through the gap in the books.

He's back to looking at his laptop.

He doesn't know I'm hiding behind here, scrutinizing and analyzing him.

Just like Tobias did to me.

A shudder runs up my spine, making the back of my neck prickle.

Look what I've turned into.

A suspicious, lurking, untrusting lunatic.

I work in a public library, and because some new guy has started coming in, I think he has an ulterior motive.

Like he's here to kill me.

Christ.

3

I have never even spoken to the guy, not even gotten within a few feet of him, and I have pegged him as a fan of Tobias Ripley's work. Or worse, a copycat, and he's come to finish the job that Tobias didn't when he left me alive that night.

I have officially lost my mind.

I step back from the stacks and press my hands to my face as I let out a breath.

I just need to get back to work, putting these returned books away, and forget all about the stranger over there.

He's not here for me.

I'm safe now.

I pick a book up from the pile of returns on the cart. Check the numbered code on the spine and slide it back into its home. Ready for someone else to check it out.

TWO

When my shift at the library is over, I walk back to my apartment. I take a leisurely stroll. I'm not in any particular rush. It's not snowing at the moment, and it's not like I have anything to get home for.

Although it might not be snowing, it's still as cold as balls here in Jackson. Typical Wyoming weather for this time of year. Not that I'm from around here. But when I moved here, I quickly learned to keep myself well wrapped up, so I wouldn't freeze to death.

It's not a way I want to die.

It's on my list, among a few other routes to death, of things I would rather avoid.

I meander down the sidewalk, and I people-watch as I go. I'm not really sure why I do it because all it does is make me feel envious of those people living their lives the way they want to. Out shopping with friends or loved ones. Couples hand in hand.

And now, all I'm reminded of is what my life used to be like before everything happened.

If you had asked me a couple of years ago where I saw myself, it sure as hell wouldn't have been here.

I decide to stop at the coffee shop I pass daily and grab a takeout hot chocolate.

I push through the door and enter the warmth of the shop. My eyes do a quick scan of the place, and I stop in my tracks.

The stranger from the library is here.

My heart does a weird jolt in my chest. I don't know why.

The stranger is sitting at a table in the back. He has a book in his hand.

My eyes travel down to the book he's holding. It's the one he checked out earlier.

I know that because I was seated at the computer near the checkout desk, looking up when a book was expected in. I surreptitiously watched while my manager, Margaret, checked his book out. They made small talk. I wasn't close enough to hear.

It was the nearest I had been to him so far.

And, yes, it is weird that I'm cataloguing these facts.

I'm starting to think I have truly lost my mind.

Or that I left it back in Chicago before I moved here.

The stranger looks up from the book in his hand, and I quickly avert my eyes, acting as though I didn't see him.

Not that he knows who I am.

You know, because I'm the weird library lurker.

My nerves are all over the place. I'm not sure why because it's not like he knows me. Or that I have seen him at the library.

I'm relieved though when my drink is ready and I can leave.

I pick up my drink, but before I make for the exit, I give one quick look in the stranger's direction.

He's staring right at me. My eyes meet with his.

My stomach flips over.

His lips tip up into a friendly smile.

I quickly look away, turn, and walk out of the coffee shop.

What the hell is wrong with me?

Why am I so affected by this guy's presence? I don't even know him!

It's ridiculous. I'm ridiculous.

The only thing I can come up with is because he's hot and I am physically attracted to him.

It has been a long time since I have felt any form of attraction to any man, so that's why my hormones are overreacting.

That is all it can be.

It's quiet outside when I let myself in my building.

I walk up the stairs to the second floor, where my apartment is.

As I turn down the hall, I see a cat sitting in the hallway.

A bad memory crawls over my skin. But I force it away.

The cat watches me approach.

It's gray and white. Fluffy. Totally adorable.

I stop when I reach it. Bend down and give it a pet. "Hey, cutie."

It meows, nuzzling its head against my hand.

"What are you doing out here, all by your lonesome?"

I look around to see if anyone else is in the hall, maybe its owner, but no sign of anyone.

I check for a collar, but it isn't wearing one.

Maybe it's a stray that got in the building.

Do I just leave it here?

It would be mean to just leave it, but my track record with cats is not good.

The last cat I liked was killed.

Because of me.

My spine stiffens. I stand abruptly and start to walk away toward my apartment.

Seconds later, guilt catches up with me, and I glance back over my shoulder.

The cat is following me.

"Oh, honey, no, you don't want to follow me. Cats and me, well, we are ..." I sigh and shake my head. "Basically, long story short, you're better off elsewhere."

And now, I'm explaining myself to a cat.

This is what solitude will do to a person.

I keep walking, and when I reach my door, the cat is next to my feet, brushing up against my leg.

"I don't have kitty food, if that's what you're thinking." I sigh down at the cat, who is just looking up at me. "The last cat I liked ... well, let me just say, it didn't work out so well for him."

The little stray meows up at me.

I sigh again and put my key in the door, unlocking it. "Well, don't say I didn't warn you."

I open the door, and the cat trots on in.

I close the door behind us and lock it. Slide the upper and lower dead bolts into place and put on the chain.

I put my bag down and then do a sweep of the apartment, like I always do. A routine I have to do every time I come home.

Checking all the rooms, every place a person could possibly hide in my small apartment. I make sure the windows are still locked. And I turn on all the lights. Even though it's still light outside, it will be dark soon, and I don't like walking into any room when it's dark.

When my search is done, I come back to the living room. The cat has made itself at home on the sofa.

I shrug off my coat, hanging it up, and kick off my shoes.

"You hungry, huh?" I walk into the kitchen. "Well, I don't have cat food. But I think I have some canned tuna."

I reach into the cupboard and get a can of tuna, hidden behind the soup.

I get a clean saucer from the dishwasher and open up the can.

The cat is up and jumping onto the counter straightaway. I probably should tell her to get down—hygiene reasons and all—but she's so lovely that I can't bring myself to.

"You hungry, cutie?" I murmur, giving the cat a stroke.

I open the can and empty it out onto the saucer. The cat is on the food immediately.

I get a small bowl and fill it with fresh water from the tap, and I place it next to the saucer of tuna.

I leave the cat eating, and I go into my bedroom and change out of my work clothes. I put on a fresh tank top, pull a T-shirt over it, and put on some sweatpants.

I head back into the living room and glance over at the cat, who is still working its way through the tuna.

Do I take it to a shelter?

But then if no one comes to claim it, they might put it down.

I can't let that happen.

I could put a poster up around the building. But that would mean giving out my cell phone number.

Definitely not happening.

What to do?

I guess I could try knocking on my neighbors' doors. The cat could belong to one of them.

Getting up, I go and retrieve my sneakers from my closet and put them on.

"I'm just going to go and see if I can find your owner," I say to the cat, like it actually knows what I'm saying or cares where I'm going.

Keys in hand, I pause at the door.

I've only been inside for a short period of time. But it doesn't matter how long it's been. I always struggle to open my front door.

Because of …

No, don't think about it.

Don't think about any of it.

I slide open the first dead bolt.

Then the second.

Unlatch the chain.

Turn the lock.

Hand on the door handle, I take a deep breath.

Nothing is there. Nothing is there. Nothing is there.

I let out the breath while pushing down on the handle, and I yank open the door.

The hallway floor outside my apartment is empty.

I close my eyes, momentarily relieved.

I step into the hall and shut the door behind me, locking it.

Then, I start the task of knocking on each of my neighbor's doors and speaking to people I have spent the last six months avoiding.

THREE

I let myself back into my apartment, locking the door behind me. The cat is sitting on the sofa, looking at me.

"Well, seems no one knows who you belong to." I shrug.

Not one of my neighbors had a clue. Except the elderly lady in apartment 212, who I learned is called Chloe, has severe arthritis, and is actually really nice. She told me that, a few days ago, a new guy had moved into apartment 209, which is down the other end of the hall from mine, so the cat could possibly be his.

But when I knocked on apartment 209's door, there was no answer. So, I'll try later.

I do my check of my apartment again.

Stupid, I know, because I was gone all of fifteen minutes, but I won't settle until I've done it.

When I'm finished, I grab the book I started last night—about a hot-as-hell hockey player and the girl he shouldn't be in love with but is.

I might not be able to have love in my life, but that doesn't mean I can't read about it.

Taking a seat on the sofa next to my new friend, I put the TV on for background noise. Total silence makes me uncomfortable.

The cat climbs into my lap and gets herself settled.

"Guess you're sitting here then."

I begin reading my book, and I stroke her soft fur, enjoying the sound of her sweet, little purring noise.

I have gotten only halfway through a chapter when there's a knock at my door, and I almost jump out of my skin.

I scare the crap out of the cat as well. It skitters to the other side of the sofa.

"Sorry," I whisper to the cat, pressing my hand to my chest against my pounding heart.

Putting my book down, I get up and walk on quiet feet to the front door.

Reaching up on my tiptoes, I peer through the peephole.

And my heart stops.

It's the guy from the library.

He's here at my front door.

I take a step back.

Why is he here?

How does he know I live here?

Blood starts to rush to my head.

I feel dizzy.

I reach for the wall for support.

Another knock.

"Hello?" His voice is deep and throaty, and it does a combination of things to me. Makes my stomach flip and my fear increase.

It's confusing to me.

What should I do?

Ignore him? Pretend that I'm not here?

"Uh, my name is Jack. I live in the building. Apartment 209. I moved in a few days ago." His voice is clear as glass through the door. "My cat got out, and our neighbor—Chloe from apartment 212—said that you found her."

A couple of things happen in this moment.

I realize that he knows I'm in here. Otherwise, he wouldn't have given me the whole spiel through the door. Which makes me feel stupid for acting like I wasn't here.

This guy lives in my building?

I've seen him at the library but not here. But to be fair, it's not like I see any of my neighbors. I make it my business not to.

And the cat is his. Which gives me a mixed feeling of relief and disappointment.

In this short time, I've really gotten to like my furry friend.

Licking my dry lips, I swallow before speaking, "Sorry. Yes. Just hold on one second."

I work my way through the locks that keep the world out and me safely inside.

I open the door, revealing him.

He's still wearing the clothes I saw him in earlier, sans the leather jacket. His hair is ruffled, like he just ran his fingers through it.

And close up, he is even better-looking.

Crap.

"Hi." He has a smile on his face, but then his expression seems to click into recognition. "Oh. Hey. You work at the library, right?"

My heart thuds in my chest.

He's seen me there.

And there I was, thinking I had been inconspicuous.

"Um … yes, I do." My words come out croaky, like I haven't spoken in years.

"Yeah, I thought I recognized you." He glances over my head into my apartment. "So, you have Eleven."

"Eleven?"

"My cat."

"Oh. Yeah. I'll just go get her for you."

I turn away, and I shut the door.

Right. In. His. Face.

It's out of habit. But also rude as hell.

I cringe.

Then, I pull the door back open and give him a sheepish look. "Sorry," I say to him.

He just laughs. It's an easygoing laugh but nice too. "No problem."

"Okay. Well, I'll just go get her."

God, I'm acting even more awkward than normal.

Remember the days when you used to be a normal person, Audrey? And also when you didn't talk to yourself in the third person?

Oh, those were the days.

Sigh.

I retrieve Eleven, as I now know her to be named, from the sofa. Holding her to me, I walk back to where Jack is waiting for us in the doorway to my apartment.

"Here she is." I hand her over to him.

Jack's hand brushes mine in the exchange. A zing of heat shoots up my arm, and my pulse increases in tempo.

It surprises me. Enough that I step back away from him.

I've never had such an instant physical reaction to a man before.

And I shouldn't be having one now.

I wrap my arms over my chest.

"Thanks," he says. "I hope she wasn't too much trouble."

"Not at all."

"I honestly have no clue how she got out of the apartment," he tells me.

"I did check for a collar on her," I feel the need to tell him. I don't want him thinking I go around, taking in stray pussies.

And thank God I didn't just say that out loud.

"Yeah, I gave up on collars a while back. She always gets them off and ditches them. She is chipped though."

"Clever cat," I muse.

"Too clever. I'm going to have to check the apartment, find where she escaped from. Whereabouts did you find her?"

"In the hallway. She followed me to my apartment. When I unlocked my door, she walked on in. I knocked on everyone's door on our floor, but no one knew who she belonged to. Well, except Chloe said she thought she might belong to you. I did try knocking on your door, but you weren't there. Obviously. I was going to try later …" I trail off, realizing I sound like a complete moron.

"I fed her too. I hope that's okay. It was just a can of tuna. It was all I had." And yet, I just can't seem to stop.

He smiles. It's warm and friendly. "That was really nice of you."

I shrug, turning my gaze down.

"Well, Eleven and I appreciate it," he adds.

"I like her name," I say, feeling like I should say something.

"*Stranger Things*," he says.

"Stranger things?" I echo.

"The TV show. Eleven is a character from it."

"Oh. Of course. Yes, I have heard of the show, but I've never watched it." I shake my head.

"You're missing out."

"Scary shows aren't really my thing." I shrug.

Honestly, I avoid watching anything remotely scary now. I have enough scary memories trapped in my head without adding to them.

"It's not scary."

"No?" I tip my head to the side in question. "What is your definition of scary?"

"*The Witches.*"

"The witches?"

"Yeah," he deadpans. "From the Roald Dahl book. Well, not the book. The movie. Those freaky, toeless, bald-headed witches used to scare the absolute shit out of me when I was a kid." He squares his shoulders. "And I am man enough to admit that they still freak me out now."

He shudders, a wry grin on his lips, and a laugh flies out of my mouth.

It shocks the hell out of me. I can't actually remember the last time I laughed.

When I was still the old me.

My laughter dies as quickly as it appeared.

I place my hand on the door, ready to close it.

He seems to understand the gesture, as he moves away. "Well, thanks again for looking out for Eleven."

"No problem." I shut the door before he even starts to walk away.

I lean back up against it and squeeze my eyes shut.

How can a laugh make me feel so off-kilter?

It's pathetic.

Not even taking into account that the whole conversation with Jack was the longest exchange that I have had with another person since I moved here.

And my weekly calls with my brother don't count.

I know it's my choice not to get close to people.

But it's the only choice.

Only ... I didn't realize until now just how starved for conversation I actually am.

And Jack seems harmless.

I bet Ted Bundy did at first too.

But do I actually think this guy is a serial killer?

No.

Possibly.

Oh, I don't know.

I don't know anything anymore.

I barely even know myself.

Sighing, I push off the door. Lock it back up. Resist the strong urge to do a check of my apartment again.

I sit back down on my sofa, pick my book up, and make a conscious effort to be a normal person while also ignoring the loneliness surrounding me, which somehow seems so much more prevalent than usual.

FOUR

"Hello again."

I jump at the sound of the deep voice behind me, the book in my hand falling to the floor.

Spinning around, I see Jack standing there.

My heart takes off for a few reasons.

Adrenaline, fear … the hot guy standing in front of me.

"Sorry. I didn't mean to scare you." Giving me a sheepish smile, he bends down, picking up the book I just dropped.

"It's fine." I shake my head. "Don't worry." My heart doesn't agree, as it currently tries to bat its way out of its cage.

Jack holds the book out for me to take. I make sure to avoid touching him in the exchange.

"I just came over because I wanted to thank you again for looking after Eleven last night."

"It was no problem at all." I clutch the book to my chest.

Then, there's this moment of silence—you know the kind.

The kind where someone needs to speak, or it will just get weird.

People hate awkwardness. It makes them uncomfortable, and they need to get as far away from it as humanly possible.

And usually, I would just continue on with the silence, allowing it to become uncomfortable, knowing the other person would make their excuses and walk away, leaving me alone. Because that's what I want.

But this time ... I don't.

I'm the one to speak. "So, how is Eleven?"

He smiles. It's wide and happy, and it gives me a pleasant feeling in my belly. I choose not to delve into the why.

"Well, she's not happy with regular old cat food now. She turned her nose up at it this morning. I think she's gotten a taste for tuna."

"Oops. Sorry." I screw up my face, apologetic.

He laughs. It's rich and warm. Like melted chocolate in my mouth.

"No need to be sorry. You did me a favor. Not many people would have looked out for her like you did."

I shrug, looking down at my feet. "Sure, they would."

"No, they wouldn't." It's the insistent tone of his voice that brings my eyes back up to his.

There is something incredibly hypnotic about his eyes. I find it hard to look away from them—and him.

The quiet between Jack and me is here again, but now, it's filled with something else ... something that I shouldn't be feeling around any man.

But I still can't seem to look away.

Thankfully, Jack breaks the spell he put me under.

"So"—he clears his throat—"I was wondering if you would let me buy you a coffee, as a thanks for taking care of Eleven yesterday."

Of course, my hormones immediately say yes.

Thankfully, my head is smarter and more in control than my long-underused female parts.

"That's not necessary. But thank you for the offer."

See, I can say no politely.

"Come on. You've got to let me do something. Buy you a takeout coffee at least?"

He pushes his hands into his jean pockets, rocking back on his heels. His smile is boyish. And the old me would have fallen for it in seconds.

Well, to be fair, the old Audrey would have said yes to the first offer of coffee, quite likely sitting in a coffee shop with him right now—or well on her way to one.

But this Audrey won't. She can't.

"Honestly, it's not necessary." I keep my face pleasant but my tone firm.

"Okay." He nods, seeming to get the hint. "But the offer stands if you ever change your mind."

I won't.

"Thanks."

His smile is congenial. "Right, well, I'll leave you in peace. Have a good rest of the day."

"You too. Have a great day, that is."

For Christ's sake. I really wish I could be normal, just for once.

Jack hesitates a moment, like he's going to say something else. I hold my breath, waiting. Wanting him to both go and stay in equal measure. It's a weird feeling for me.

Usually, all I want is for people to leave me alone.

With him … it's definitely mixed.

I want to push him away with one hand and pull him back with the other.

It's confusing and disconcerting. I have known the guy not even twenty-four hours.

Okay, I was maybe watch-stalking him for a little longer than that.

But that doesn't mean I know him because I most definitely do not.

You never really know anyone.

"So, I'll see you around, Audrey," he says.

The feelings his deep voice elicits in me have me turning away from him, giving him my back. "Probably not. Bye, Jack."

I sound like a bitch. But it's best he thinks of me as one.

I don't need Jack to think we're neighbors who can chat.

Yes, we might be neighbors, but my avoidance skills are second to none. If avoiding people were an Olympic sport, I would be a gold medalist.

I lift the book in my hand, ready to put it back in its place on the shelf.

I hear Jack sigh softly behind me, followed by the sound of his footsteps as he walks away, leaving me alone.

Alone, like I want to be.

FIVE

I stare down at the silent cell phone in my hand.

I used to have a phone that rang often. Dinged with text messages. Social media notifications.

I had friends. A life.

Now, I have a phone that stays silent. No text messages from friends. No social media accounts, as I deleted them all.

I have no friends. No life.

I basically have this cell phone in case of emergency and so I can call my brother, Cole.

I have to call him once a week to check in. It was our agreement when I told him I was moving away from the only home I had ever known.

I bring the screen to life and dial Cole's number.

He answers on the second ring.

The sound of his voice saying, "Hi," fills my chest with warmth.

It's that feeling of home. Only my brother can give me that feeling now.

"Hey," I say to him. "How are you doing?"

"I'm good. Miss my sister. Wish she would let me see her."

"Cole ..." I sigh.

"I know; I know," he utters. "I just think it's crazy that you won't let me see you. Even crazier is that you won't tell me where you are."

"Can we not go over this again?" We have this exact same conversation every single time we speak. "You know my reasoning."

Cole doesn't know where I am. I didn't tell him when I left.

It's not that I don't trust him; of course I do. He is the only person in the whole world I do trust. I just worry if he came to visit me here, and he was followed ...

A shudder runs through me.

After the murders and Tobias's trial, Chicago just didn't feel like home anymore. There was the press, constantly outside my house, and then there were the crazies, fans of Tobias. I guess I just didn't feel safe in Chicago any longer.

I wanted to get away from people. Including my brother. I know that sounds awful, and I would never say it to him out loud. And it's not that I don't love him or want to be around him ... but I just wanted a fresh start.

To be somewhere no one knew me or about what had happened.

"Just because I know your reasoning doesn't mean that I agree with it. But fine, I will never bring it up again." His tone is annoyed. It's been like that a lot recently when we talk. And he also says that every time we speak—that he won't bring it up again, but he always does.

But I can't be angry with him. He's done so much for me. Taken care of me my entire life.

"Thank you," I say softly, trying to appease the situation, not wanting the only family I have left to be angry with me. "So, what have you been up to since we last spoke?"

"Just the usual. Work. Go to the gym. Got a haircut yesterday."

"You change the style? Dye it? Let me guess … you got a blue Mohawk."

He chuckles, and the sound makes me smile.

"Nothing that interesting. Just a trim."

"Damn. I think you would rock a blue Mohawk."

"Hardly." He laughs again.

My brother is a handsome guy. Dark brown hair, brown eyes, six feet tall.

We don't look much alike.

"Have you been to the cemetery recently?" I ask him.

Our adoptive parents died in a car accident. Just before Tobias made his appearance in my life.

"No." His answer is short and blunt.

Cole doesn't like to talk about our parents' deaths. Their deaths hit him hard. They hit me hard too. Losing them was devastating. I loved them so much.

Cole and I haven't been lucky … if that's the right word … when it comes to parents.

Our biological parents died when I was four and Cole was eight. They were murdered.

I don't recall much about them, only the vague memory of what they looked like. But Cole remembers them. Not that he will talk to me about them either.

I think it's harder for him because he has those memories of our biological parents.

Cole has lost two sets of parents that he loved. And I'm sure I would have loved our biological parents too. But it's hard to mourn what you barely remember.

After our parents were gone, we were placed in a foster home, and we were lucky to both be adopted by our foster parents. Not many kids in the foster system get to stay with siblings. Honestly, I don't think I would have coped without Cole.

Well, I know I wouldn't have coped without him. He's definitely the stronger of the two of us.

But it wasn't until Tobias that I started to think that maybe I was cursed. First, my biological parents had been murdered. Then, my adoptive parents had died. Then, Tobias started stalking me and killing people.

Death follows me around; that's for sure.

I think that Cole is safer, not being around me. Not that I would tell him this. He'd just say I was thinking crazy.

"I'm sorry if I upset you," I say softly.

"You didn't. I just don't like talking about … them."

And that's why I ask, why I bring them up. Because I don't think it's healthy, not to talk about things.

But still, I say, "I know. I'm sorry."

"Stop saying sorry and tell me what you've been up to this week. And don't give me the same *nothing* answer that you give me every week."

"Actually, I—" I'm about to tell him about the cat and then stop. Because that conversation would lead to

Jack, and for some reason, I really don't want to tell him about Jack.

My brother is overprotective of me. He always has been. I think that's why he finds it hard, not knowing where I am.

I know if I tell him about Jack, he'll worry.

Not that there is anything to worry about.

I think.

"You what?" he prompts.

I quickly change gears. "I went to the grocery store yesterday. They had those Caramel Apple Pops that we were obsessed with when we were kids. You remember them?"

"Yeah, I do," he says.

I can hear the smile in his voice, and I'm glad that I put it there even if it was due to a lie.

It is scary to me just how quickly I pulled that lie about Caramel Apple Pops out of the air. I don't even know if you can still buy them, to be honest. But I won't overthink it.

"So, yeah, I grabbed a handful of them. They're gone already." I laugh. "And I checked out a new book from work, so I've been reading that. What else? Oh, I started a new show on Netflix called *Stranger Things*."

Okay, so I got curious about it after Jack said how good it was.

It's not been too scary so far. But I am only two episodes in.

Plenty of time to change my mind on it.

"I've never watched it," Cole tells me.

"Not your kind of thing, to be fair."

Cole is more of a movie watcher, usually action films rather than TV shows. I love a good binge-watch of a new television show.

"So, have you made any new friends?" he asks me.

That comes out of left field. Cole knows my reason for coming out here was to be alone. That making friends is not part of my plan.

I'm trying to not freak out that he asked the question. But it's weird that I have only recently just met Jack and then Cole asks me that.

Not that Jack and I are friends.

Far from it.

Either it's a coincidence or my brother is psychic.

I don't believe in coincidences, so I'm going with psychic. He always does seem to know my business.

"Nope." I let the *P* pop. *I'm not fessing up to him, psychic or not.* "You know that I'm not here to make friends."

"I know. I just wondered if that had changed. You can't stay away from people forever, Audrey."

"Yes, I can."

He sighs. "Isn't there anyone at work who you talk with?"

Not more than a few sentences.

"Nope. That's the beauty of working in a library. It's silent. No one talks."

"Audrey …"

"And anyway, I don't need anyone, except for my big brother."

There's silence, and if I couldn't hear him breathing, I would think the line had been cut.

"You know I love you, right?"

I smile. "Love you too, Cole. I'm going to head off now. A hot bath is calling my name."

"Call me in a week."

It's not a request.

I roll my eyes, not that he can see, and say, "Yes, Drill Sergeant."

Cole laughs. We say our good-byes, and I hang up the phone.

I go straight to the bathroom and put the tub plug in. After turning the hot and cold taps on, I pour some bubble bath in.

I wander into my bedroom, tossing my cell onto the bed. I lift my top, ready to take it off, when I hear a noise that stops me dead in my tracks.

Slowly, I lower my top back down and strain my ears to listen over the sound of the running taps.

It's like ... a tapping ... no, a scratching noise.

Cold slivers down my spine.

My head swivels, my eyes looking around my bedroom and my ears trying to locate the source of the sound.

But it's hard when my pulse is pounding loudly along with my heart.

I reach out, grabbing my cell off the bed. Pressing the off button to bring up the emergency call service.

It sounds like it's coming from the living room.

Phone in hand, I walk quietly down the hall, going toward the living room, in the direction of the sound.

My eyes zero in on the front door.

The noise is coming from there.

Someone is outside my door.

Shit.

A dozen memories assault my mind, making me feel sick and dizzy.

Not again. Please not again.

Calm down, Audrey. Tobias is in prison.
You're safe. It is not happening again.
Scratch. Scratch.
I need to just check this out.
It's probably nothing.

Hand curled around my phone, I walk on silent feet to the door. Rise up on my tiptoes and look through the peephole.

The hallway is empty.

Scratch. Scratch.

I jump back. Heart pounding.

Jesus.

I need to call the police.

And say what?

There's a scratching noise outside my door. Please come quickly.

I would sound like a crazy person.

I am a crazy person.

And it's not like I can call anyone to come check it out.

The only person I have is Cole, and he is hundreds of miles away with no clue as to where I am.

Well done, Audrey.

I could just ignore it.

I could just sit on the sofa and wait it out.

I have lived through this crap once. I know not what to do.

But …

I still have to know.

If someone has somehow found me.

If this has anything to do with Tobias.

I have to know.

For fuck's sake.

I really hate me sometimes.

Keeping a firm hold on my cell, my finger hovers close to the emergency button.

I open the dead bolts, one after the other.

Please don't let this be starting again.

I unlatch the chain and turn the lock.

The click sounds loud in the silence. I hear it over the pulse beating in my ears.

I take hold of the door handle.

One. Two. Three.

I push down and yank open the door.

And something runs past me, bumping against my leg.

"Argh!" I yelp, tossing my phone in the air.

Eleven.

It's the damn cat.

All that stress, and it was a cat scratching on my front door.

I let out a laugh that is half-relief, half-embarrassment at my own behavior.

Jesus, I'm such a mess.

"Christ, Eleven."

She's already sitting up on my sofa, looking pleased with herself.

"You scared the crap out of me." I run a hand over my hair. Grab my phone off the floor, push it in my back pocket, and shut the door, locking it.

I walk over to the sofa and pick her up. "What the heck are you doing out again? Where's your dad, huh?"

She purrs and nuzzles my face.

"It's a good thing you're cute," I tell her. "Come on. Let's go take you back to your dad."

I make sure to go turn the bath taps off. The last thing I need is to flood my apartment.

The trepidation is still there when I open the door to exit my apartment. I think it will always be there.

I lock up and head for Jack's apartment.

I'm going to see Jack.

A frisson of excitement bounces around in my stomach.

I immediately squash it down.

I'm just going to return Eleven and then go back to my apartment and finally take my bath.

I notice Jack's apartment door is slightly ajar as I approach.

My heart stills at the same time my legs do.

Seriously, isn't one stressful situation at a time enough?

Okay, so it was the cat.

And it could be the cat again. Maybe she let herself out of the apartment.

Cats can do that, right? Open doors and shit? They're smart. And Eleven is definitely smart.

"Did you open the door, Eleven?" I look down at her, like she's actually going to answer me.

Her response is to butt my chin with her head.

I take a deep breath and walk toward Jack's door, stopping before it.

"Hello?" I call out. "Jack? You there?"

Nothing. It's silent in his apartment too. No sounds coming from there at all.

"Why me, huh?" I say to Eleven, who looks as if she has zero cares in the world—and she has exactly that because she's a cat.

Frigging wish I were a cat right now.

Stepping closer to the door, I push it open with the hand not holding Eleven.

"Jack!" I call out.

No answer.

"For fuck's sake," I mutter. "Looks like I'm going in."

I don't have my rape alarm on me.

My phone is in my pocket though. I get it out and get it ready for a call to 911 if necessary.

One day into knowing Jack, and look what's happening already.

My life has been peaceful these past six months. And now, it's been disrupted by a cute cat and her hot owner.

Listen to me. Potentially dangerous situation, and I'm thinking about Jack being hot.

I need my head checked.

Nothing new there.

Taking a deep breath, I step inside Jack's apartment.

His apartment mirrors mine.

Except there are boxes in his living room. He did say he moved in a short time ago. A brown leather sofa. A large screen TV sitting on a wooden sideboard.

"Jack," I call out again.

Still nothing.

I walk carefully through the living room, heading to the small hall that I know will lead to the bedroom and bathroom.

Both doors are open.

One wide open, showing me it's the bathroom, and it's empty of Jack.

The other, only slightly ajar.

Which is his bedroom.

I knock on the door. "Jack?"

Still no answer.

I slowly push open the door with my hand.

The bedroom is empty too.

"Why are you in my apartment?" The deep voice comes from behind me.

I simultaneously scream and spin on the spot. In turn causing Eleven to freak out. She ejects from my arms and bolts. I feel a sharp pain on my arm. But my heart is beating too hard, adrenaline rushing through my body too quickly for me to pay it any attention.

"Jesus! Jack!" I press my hand to my chest. I'm panting, out of breath, like I just ran a marathon.

Jack is staring at me with a mixture of amusement curling his mouth and apprehension in his eyes.

Which makes sense. Because he just found his neighbor, whom he met only yesterday, standing in his bedroom.

"S-sorry," I stammer. "Eleven was at my door, scratching it, and I was ju-just bringing her back to you. Your door was open, and I called your name, but you didn't answer. I was worried, so I came in to check that you weren't hurt or anything. I'm sorry."

"Don't be. It's not every day I come home to find a pretty girl in my bedroom."

Unease slides down my spine, freezing my body up, at the same time my brain registers that Jack thinks I'm pretty.

The unease must show on my face though because the smile on his face disappears, and he's quick to say, "Sorry, that was a bad pun."

"Oh. Oh, okay. Right." I fidget nervously. "Will Eleven be okay?"

"Yeah. She'll be fine now. Not much fazes her."

He backs up, walking out of his bedroom, and I follow him through to the living room.

And there, chilling on the sofa, is Eleven.

"Told you." He smiles in the direction of his cat.

I look over at Eleven. "Sorry I scared you, cutie."

"I thought I had shut the door," Jack says to me, heading into the open-plan kitchen. "I must not have latched it properly."

My legs stop in the living room, but my eyes follow him to the kitchen. "You didn't lock it?" I ask, confused.

"No." He shakes his head. "I just popped downstairs to see Mr. McCluskey."

Mr. McCluskey is the live-in handyman in our apartment building.

There used to be a time when I would have left the door unlocked to *pop downstairs*. Back when I feared nothing because I didn't know better.

Now, I fear everything, and I can't even step out into the hall without locking up behind me.

"The shower has been acting up," he continues, reaching into a cupboard and pulling out two mugs. "Can I get you a coffee? Tea?" He holds the mugs up.

"Oh. Erm …"

If I take a drink, then I'll have to stay. Sit down. Make conversation. Talk about myself. He might ask questions …

"No, thank you. I should get back." I'm already walking to the door.

"Oh. Okay. Sure." He seems surprised by my answer.

Maybe he's used to women wanting to stay around him. I would if I were still the old Audrey. I would have even had my flirt on the moment I met him. But not now.

I'm not even sure I know how to flirt anymore.

"Well, thanks for looking out for Eleven. Again," he adds.

I pause by the now-closed door and glance over at him. He's leaning against the kitchen countertop, facing me.

"It's fine." I tuck some stray hairs behind my ear.

"You're bleeding." Jack is already moving toward me, concern etched on his face.

"Huh?" I lower my arm, twisting it around, and see a big scratch down the outer side of my forearm, blood trickling from it.

Before I register what is actually happening, Jack takes ahold of my arm, cupping the elbow in his hand, his other hand curled around mine, and he guides me to the kitchen.

I try not to pay attention to how large his hand is, compared to mine. Or how it feels to have his skin touching mine.

Jack is touching me.

"I'm okay. Really." I try to tug my arm free, but he keeps a firm but gentle hold of it.

"Let me clean you up. Eleven must have scratched you when I scared you both."

"It was my fault. I screamed and scared her. I shouldn't have been in here—"

His eyes fix on mine. My heart jumps into my throat.

"You were being a good person." He squeezes my elbow and then releases his hold on me. "Just wait there a second."

I watch, a little dumbstruck, as he backs up out of the kitchen and goes into the living room. I want to tell him that I'm not a good person. I'm the kind of person who gets people murdered.

Jack rummages around in one of the boxes and pulls out a first aid kit a few moments later.

I avert my eyes as he walks back to me, pretending like I find the floor insanely fascinating.

He stops in front of me, putting the first aid kit on the counter beside me.

God, he smells good. Like the outdoors. Cedar wood and something inherently male.

My ovaries shimmy with happiness.

Down, girls. It ain't happening.

He rips open an antiseptic wipe, bringing my eyes to his hands and forearms. They're strong and tanned.

He takes hold of my arm again. "This will sting."

I lift my eyes to his face. His eyes are already on mine.

My heart putters to a stop.

"You ready?" he asks me.

All I can do is nod.

The first brush of the wipe over the cut stings like a bitch, but I take it like a woman.

I have experienced far worse than this in the past.

"Okay?" he checks as he continues to wipe over the scratch.

I find my voice and answer, "Yes." Although it comes out sounding a little hoarse.

He lifts my arm up, examining it. And I can't stop looking at his face. It's like I no longer have control over my eyes.

"The scratch is too long to put a Band-Aid on," he tells me. "So, you'll have to leave it uncovered. I just wanted to get it cleaned up fast, make sure it doesn't get infected."

His eyes flick to mine, and I look away, caught.

My pulse is pounding, and I can feel my cheeks starting to heat. "I'll be fine."

I tug my arm free, and he lets it go this time.

"Thank you ... for helping me with the scratch." I skirt around him, ensuring not to touch one single part of his body with mine.

"No problem." His voice hits my back as I head for the door.

I pull it open and walk through it, closing it behind me.

I practically sprint to my apartment. Let myself inside and lock up behind me.

I fall back against the door.

Jesus. I'm such a freak. I didn't even say good-bye. Just hightailed it out of there.

Jack must think I'm a crazy person.

Good. It's good if he thinks that.

Then, he'll stay away, and that is what I want.

Right?

Right.

On a sigh, I push off the door and go and do my usual check of my apartment before I continue with running my bath.

SIX

My eyes sweep up and down him. He's wearing that beaten leather jacket that he always wears. Dark blue jeans. A gray henley shirt. Biker boots on his feet.

He looks hot, like usual.

It's disconcerting, to say the least.

So is the fact that I'm seeing him again.

It was only yesterday when I was in his apartment.

He sees me, eyes locking on to mine, and smiles.

"Hi again," he says, approaching me.

"Why is it that, less than a week ago, I had never seen you before, and now, I can't go anywhere without seeing you?"

He stops a few feet from me. Lips parted slightly, like I've shocked him into silence.

Did I actually just say that?

I couldn't have just said hello and been on my way?

But seriously, I go from never seeing this guy to seeing him wherever I go.

It's ... weird.

And I have lived weird, so I know what to look for. And it's this.

He's at my place of work—it's a public building, but that doesn't count. My apartment building—okay, he lives there, too, so I'll give him that. But the coffee shop and now the grocery store?

I can go weeks. Months. Without seeing the same person again.

Granted, I avoid people at all costs.

But him? He is everywhere I go.

They're either coincidences—and I'm not a big believer in that—or he's following me.

So, I have to go with, he's following me.

Look … I know I'm a suspicious person nowadays. But come on. Any normal person would feel creeped out by this, wouldn't they?

Or was that just incredibly rude of me?

He cleaned my arm up yesterday after Eleven scratched it. He didn't have to do that.

God, I'm such a bitch.

If my adoptive mom could hear me now, she would be so disappointed.

Ashamed, I wince, my eyes closing briefly before opening back up. I look him in the eye. "That was really rude of me. I apologize."

His eyes are watchful, appraising. Like he's making his mind up about something. Quite likely me and whether he thinks I'm a dick. It would be no surprise if he thought I was a dick.

"Don't apologize. It was honest. I like honesty in a person. And I agree; it is odd that we keep running into each other. Do you believe in fate, Audrey?"

Every time he says my name, I feel … shook. Like I was just swept up by a wave and tossed around in the sea, swallowing a mouthful of salt water just for good measure.

I shake my head by way of an answer. My mouth isn't working right this second.

He grins. "Me either. We'll just call it coincidence then."

"I don't believe in that either."

His eyes move over my face before settling back on my eyes. "No?"

"Nope. Rarely is anything a coincidence."

"Rarely?" he queries.

He's so damn sharp. Picks up on everything.

"Never," I correct.

"Okay. So, what is your theory as to why we keep running into each other?"

"Because you're following me?" It comes out more like a question than a statement.

And laughter bursts from him.

He has a great laugh.

Deep and throaty. It makes him even better-looking, and until this moment, I didn't think that was possible.

His blue eyes are alight with pure humor. "So, I'm stalking you?" he says, still laughing.

I shrug. "I don't know. You tell me." Surprisingly, I'm smiling when I say this, and stalking is definitely no laughing matter to me.

"No. I'm not stalking or following you." He's still smiling. His full lips tipped up at one corner.

I want to bite those lips.

And where the hell did that thought come from?

"I could say the same about you. That you're following me." His brow lifts.

And it's my turn to laugh. "I'm really not."

"No? Why should I believe you?" He throws back at me with a smile in his eyes.

"Ditto."

"This could go on a while, huh?"

"Yep." I stubbornly jut my chin out.

Another smile, this one actually on his lips. "Okay. So, why don't we agree that neither of us is following the other? And I know that you don't believe in fate or coincidence, but that doesn't mean they don't exist. So, we'll settle on that. What do you say?"

I lift a shoulder. "I can … do that."

"Good." His voice is softer now, and his eyes linger on mine, longer than acceptable for two people who are barely even acquaintances.

I can feel things starting to heat and tighten inside of me. Things that have been dormant for a long, long time.

Things that have no business coming to life.

Still, I can't seem to stop them or shut them down. And the longer I stand here with him, staring into his eyes, the harder it is to remember why I'm not supposed to feel anything.

"Go out with me? For dinner or even just a coffee. I still owe you one, remember?"

The words out of his mouth … the softly spoken words, said in that rough-sounding voice of his, are like being hit with hot and cold water at the same time.

They wake me up from whatever spell I was letting my hormones lure me under.

"No. I can't." I take a big step back from him. "I'm sorry."

"Don't be sorry. Shit." He rubs a hand over his face. "It's my fault. I misread things."

The expression on his face. He looks … uncomfortable, awkward.

He's probably not used to being turned down. A guy with a face like his … I can't imagine it ever happening.

No woman in her right mind would ever say no to a coffee date with Jack.

But I'm not a normal woman.

I hate that I can't have those things that I once took for granted. I hate that my life is this way. But it is. And there isn't a damn thing I can do to change it.

I wish I could tell him that he hadn't misread anything. I do. I would love to go out for dinner with him. When I was the old Audrey, I would have taken him on that dinner and more. But now … I can't.

I won't.

"I should go." I start to leave, but he says my name.

And that has me turning back.

"Friends?" He gives me a tentative smile.

I briefly close my eyes, wishing I could do at least that.

I stare past him. I can't bring myself to look him in the face. This guy has an effect on me. I have never been so affected by a man before. And why I am now with him, I'm not sure.

That is something for me to figure out later—when I'm back at my apartment, alone.

"I don't … have friends."

His brows pull together. "You don't have friends?" he echoes my words back to me.

I shake my head. "It's just ..." I push a hand through my hair, releasing a sigh. "I'm not someone you want to be around."

And with that, I pivot on my heel and walk away from him.

He doesn't call me back this time.

And I can't decide if I'm relieved or disappointed.

SEVEN

MURDERED FEMALE FOUND

The body of twenty-five-year-old bar worker Natalie Jenkins was found in her apartment late last night. Sources say she was stabbed to death.

After not coming in to work for her shift and not being able to get ahold of her, concerned staff had called the police.

Police are not saying if Natalie's case is linked to the murder of twenty-six-year-old veterinarian nurse Molly Hall, who was found dead in her apartment three months ago, her throat slit and her body mutilated.

We'll update as we learn more on the story.

I stare at the words on my laptop screen, them screaming and jumping out at me in the silence of my apartment.

An icy chill slithers down my spine.

That is the second woman who has gone missing since I moved here six months ago. Both found murdered.

I had been here three months when Molly Hall disappeared. I followed the story in the beginning because it unnerved me—for obvious reasons due to my past experience with Tobias.

Aside from the fact that Molly looked similar to me, it was the way she had been killed.

Tobias liked knives. It was his weapon of choice.

Throat slit. Body mutilated.

That is exactly how Tobias killed all the women back in Chicago.

He would break into their apartments and wait for them to come home. Then, he would attack.

I get the bitter taste of bile in my mouth, feeling nauseous, just like I do every time I think of anything related to what Tobias put those women through—his sick, twisted way of getting my attention or whatever the hell he was doing.

I never understood any of it. I still don't.

But I guess no one can understand the mind of a psychopath, except the man himself.

Not that Tobias has ever admitted to any of his gruesome crimes. He maintains his innocence to this day. He currently has his lawyers working on an appeal to try and get him out of prison.

Jesus, I can't even think about what I would do if he ever managed to get out of jail …

I press my hand to the upper part of my stomach, feeling the familiar scars he left there.

It won't happen. He won't get out of jail.

I'm safe.

And there is zero evidence to say that Natalie Jenkins's murder has any link to Molly's. Just because those two women were murdered, stabbed to death, does not mean that another serial killer is on the loose or that those women's deaths are at all connected to the crimes that Tobias committed.

He has been in prison for a year. These women were murdered during that time.

And people are killed every single day in America. It's an awful fact, but it's true.

Knife crime is high.

Nothing in that news story says Natalie's murder was the exact same as Molly's.

In fact, it says Natalie was stabbed to death and that Molly had her throat slit and her body mutilated. If anything, Molly's murder is closer to Tobias's method, but that still doesn't mean it has anything to do with his previous crimes.

Each woman could have been murdered by an ex-boyfriend, a family member, or a friend. Something like eighty percent of people are murdered by someone they know.

Yes, the murders of those women are similar to the killings of Tobias Ripley—both killed by knives in their apartments.

But the same could be said of a lot of murders.

Yes, Molly Hall looked a lot like me, but that means nothing.

And I have no idea what Natalie looked like. They didn't show a picture of her with the news story.

What if she looked like me?

Fuck.

I shouldn't look her up. I know this. But still, I can't stop myself.

Self-control has never been a strength of mine.

I'm already opening up a fresh window, bringing up Google and typing *Natalie Jenkins* in the search bar, before I can think again about why this is a bad idea.

The screen fills with links. I click on the Images tab, and the first row of pictures shows photos of the same girl. She has dark brown hair.

Please be her.

I click on the picture and find her Facebook page. It's private, so I can only see the profile picture.

Unsure if this is the right Natalie Jenkins, I type *murdered* next to her name in the search bar. Several other news stories come up, and a couple of them include a picture.

I click on one, and it's the same picture from her Facebook page.

So, it's definitely her, and she has shoulder-length dark brown hair.

A sense of relief fills my chest.

Which makes me feel shitty.

This girl lost her life, and I'm relieved that she had brown hair.

It's just … Tobias would only kill girls who fit my physical description. He never deviated from that. The girls always had long blonde hair, like mine, and blue eyes.

And, yes, I know Tobias is locked up, so it couldn't have been him. But I have a fear that Tobias will somehow get someone to come here and kill me. Or worse ... there's a copycat killer, and it will start all over again.

But with Natalie having dark brown hair, it means it couldn't have anything to do with Tobias. If someone were following Tobias's rules, the victim wouldn't have dark hair. She would be blonde, like me.

And Molly was murdered months ago, and nothing weird has happened to me. No love notes, no dead animals left outside my door for me to find. No notes left on any dead bodies, addressed to me.

The first woman Tobias murdered, he left a piece of paper on the body with my name written clearly on it, stating that he had killed her for me. He left it unsigned though.

Always unsigned.

Like the note on the second body that he left for me.

After the third murder, he stopped leaving notes for me, but the police, the press, and I knew that those women—those innocent women whose lives he had snuffed out—were another of his gifts for me.

Why?

I don't think I will ever know.

And I'm not sure I want to.

I let out a breath, my head dropping onto the back of the sofa.

I have got to stop this crap. I really need to quit torturing myself in this way. And I have to stop looking for similarities in every death or murder that happens, in fear that they are somehow similar to what Tobias did. Worrying that it's one of his fans—yes, the guy has fans. I need to stop fearing that another sicko is going to come and finish the job that Tobias started.

Why didn't he kill me that night?

It's the one question in all of this that tortures and haunts me. The one thing I can't get away from to this day. The thing that I will never understand.

I was supposed to be Tobias's finale. Everything he had done … was building up to me.

Not that he ever told me that.

I came to that conclusion myself. I mean, what else could all of it have been for?

The night he took me … he didn't speak a word to me. Not one single word.

I never saw his face.

But I felt him. Felt the blade that he used to cut my skin.

Mine.

That word forever scarred on my body.

Chills cover me, sinking into my bones. My hand instinctively covers my scars again.

I remember the pain. How much it hurt.

How I thought I was going to die.

I can feel my anxiety rising.

My breath starts to come out in quick pants.

Stop.

I press the heels of my hands to my eyes, trying to block out the memories, forcing my breaths to slow down.

Deep breath in through the nose. Out slowly through the mouth.

And repeat.

I'm safe.

No one is going to hurt me.

I'm safe.

I used to have panic attacks regularly after the murders, but they abated when I moved here.

When I stopped thinking about everything that had happened all the damn time. Letting it control every aspect of my life.

Letting Tobias still control my life.

He has no power over me.

I'm the only person who has power over me.

I have worked hard on myself to get to where I am. I'm not going backward.

I have control over that. What I allow myself to do. Think. Or feel.

I am in total control.

Deep breath in through the nose. Out slowly through the mouth.

And repeat.

I'm safe.

No one is going to hurt me.

I'm safe.

What happened is in the past. It's over.

Tobias is in prison.

End of story.

I slam my laptop shut.

The murders of those two women have nothing to do with what happened to me, and they have no connection to Tobias Ripley whatsoever.

They are terrible and tragic. And I hope and pray that their killers are brought to justice and punished.

But those murders—or any, for that matter—are not something I need to think about. Or look into in any way, shape, or form.

Pushing my laptop aside onto the sofa, I get up and head to the kitchen to get a drink.

I reach into the fridge and grab a Diet Coke, slamming the door shut. I get some chips from the cupboard, flop back down on the sofa, pick up the remote, and turn on Netflix. It comes up with *Stranger Things* as last watched, and my mind instantly goes to Jack.

Then, I remember what happened the previous time I saw him, and I shut that thought down.

Nope. Not going there.

I'm not thinking about Jack or anyone else tonight.

And sorry, Stranger Things, *but I can't watch you right now.*

I search for a comedy, needing to fill my mind with humor so I don't think about anything related to my past.

I will sit here and pretend that I am a normal twenty-four-year-old who watches movies at home with chips for company and is … well, completely normal.

EIGHT

I haven't seen Jack at the library for the past several days. Four, to be exact. He was coming in every day, regular as clockwork, and now, nothing.

I haven't bumped into him anywhere or seen him around our apartment building. Not that I used to see him there, but ...

It's like he's avoiding me.

And it bothers me for several reasons.

Firstly, I've noticed his absence from my life. The little that he's actually been in it.

I shouldn't be noticing him—or anyone. But I have, and that fact irritates the hell out of me.

Secondly, I think the reason Jack is avoiding me is because he asked me out and I said no. And also because I told him that we couldn't be friends. Because I'm nice like that.

God, I'm such a bitch.

He's literally stopped coming to the library to do whatever the hell it was that he did on his laptop all day and disappeared out of my life as quickly as he appeared in it—right after that awkward-as-hell moment in the supermarket.

When I repeat the whole conversation back in my head, it sounds awful.

And it wasn't the first time that I was a bitch to him.

Sure, I can't be friends with the guy. I can't be friends with anyone. But there are better ways to handle things than the way I did.

I could have said, *Sure, friends.*

It wouldn't have meant I had to actually do anything with him. It wouldn't have meant we had to be besties and sit around and braid each other's hair.

When he said friends, he probably meant in the acquaintance, friendly way.

I should have just said yes.

Then, I wouldn't feel like such a dick, and I wouldn't be obsessing about it right now.

I know I should just sort this out.

But I can't go actively seek him out because that would be weird and probably give him the wrong message.

If I could accidentally run into him again, maybe I could say something then.

But that's not looking likely at the moment. Not now that he's avoiding me and now that whatever had us running into each other all the time has decided to stop.

I either shut the fuck up about it and move on. Or go knock on his door after work tonight and apologize for my terrible behavior.

I've got the rest of the afternoon to figure out what I want to do.

But right now, I'm going on my lunch break.

Instead of eating in the break room, I decide to go wild and go out to grab some food.

I'm heading out to the coffee shop I like to go to. They have the most amazing cinnamon-and-raisin bagels, and I have been craving one since I woke up this morning.

I'm still deciding whether to get takeout or stay in when I walk inside and see Jack sitting at one of the tables in the corner. His laptop opened in front of him.

And that for sure answers my question as to whether he's been staying away from the library on purpose.

As if sensing me, he lifts his eyes from his screen and locks on to mine straightaway.

There's a wariness to them that I haven't seen before. And I'm the one who put it there.

Guilt lodges in my chest. I really hate the feeling.

It's an emotion that's been torturing me for the last few years.

I try to push the guilt away, but it's not budging.

I guess this is my moment to decide what to do. The afternoon that I thought I had to figure it out has now become seconds.

And I am well aware that I'm standing stock-still in the entryway of the coffee shop, staring at Jack across the room.

I don't know why I'm struggling with this so much.

Make a decision. Go over and apologize or don't.

It's that simple.

Only … it doesn't feel that simple for some reason.

It feels … significant somehow.

In a way I can't describe.

But I also know that I have to go over and apologize because if I don't, I'll just annoy myself further, obsessing over this.

Just go over, say sorry for being a dick, and go.

I take a deep breath and move my feet in Jack's direction.

I can hear "Incomplete" by Backstreet Boys playing in the background, and it sounds like the soundtrack to my life.

Jack's eyes hold mine the whole time I walk toward him.

It's unnerving. I feel like he can see all the thoughts in my head and all the shame in my soul. I want to cut eye contact, but I can't seem to. Or I don't want to. I haven't figured out which one it is yet.

"Hi," I say, reaching his table.

"Hello," he says in a low, husky voice.

Shivers ripple over my skin at the sound of him.

I grit my teeth, ignoring the sensation.

It's only been four days, and I'm getting shivery over the sound of his voice. It drives me nuts, the effect he has on me. One *hello* from him, and my ovaries do backflips.

"So …" I say, not really sure what to say now that I'm here, standing in front of him.

"So …" he echoes, leaning back in his chair.

What to say? What to say?

"You can still use the library, you know. You don't have to avoid me."

His eyes widen a fraction, like he wasn't expecting that to come out of my mouth. Neither was I. But I've said it now. There's no taking it back and going with something else.

Jack's head tips to the side, just a fraction. His hair tumbles over his forehead. I have this sudden, weird urge to reach over and push his hair back off his face. It's like an itch in my hand.

I grip the back of the chair in front of me to stop myself from doing it.

"Who says I'm avoiding you?" Jack says evenly.

"The fact that, before, I couldn't turn a corner without seeing you, and now, you're nowhere to be seen."

He lets out a laugh, which catches the attention of a few people seated around us.

"Fair enough," he says without seeming to notice or care that people are looking at him.

And I smile. I can't help it.

"So, you are avoiding me?" I push.

He says nothing. Just holds my stare.

I'm the first to break it. I look down at the table, letting out a sigh. "I'm sorry that I was a bitch the other day."

"I didn't think you were being a bitch."

I bring my eyes back to his. But I can't get a read on him. There's nothing in his expression to tell me whether he truly meant what he said or if he was just being polite.

"Well, you thought something. Enough to sit in a coffee shop with your laptop to avoid seeing me. And … I, uh … feel bad."

A smile appears in his eyes, and it warms my chest.

"You feel bad because I'm sitting in a nice, warm coffee shop?"

"No. Yes. No." I press my fingertips to my forehead, trying to gather my suddenly scattered thoughts. This guy has a way of making me feel flustered and confused at the drop of a hat. It's disconcerting. "I feel bad because you *feel* like you can't come to the library because I'm there. Because of what happened … you know … at the supermarket."

He sighs and sits forward, pushing down the lid of his laptop, resting his hands on top of it. "Look, Audrey, truth is, I wasn't avoiding you. I was just trying to give you a little space. I didn't want you feeling uncomfortable at your place of work because of me."

"You wouldn't have made me feel uncomfortable."

He gives me a knowing look, telling me he's aware that he makes me feel uncomfortable.

He does but not for the reasons he thinks.

It's because I'm attracted to him … well, *attraction* is maybe too tame a word for what I feel when I'm around this guy.

"Okay," I concede. "I would have felt a tad uncomfortable for about thirty seconds, and then I would have been fine."

He laughs a low sound, and I feel it in my chest and between my legs. The urge to press my thighs together is real.

"Are you staying?" he asks me.

"I haven't decided," I answer truthfully.

"I was just going to get another coffee. Why don't you let me buy you one—in a takeout cup? And then you can decide to stay or not …" He lets his words hang.

I hesitate.

Jesus, it's just coffee. That I can take with me if I want to. It's not like I'm making besties with the guy.

"Okay." I find myself nodding my agreement. "But I was also going to grab a cinnamon-and-raisin bagel."

Smiling, he stands. "I'll get that in a takeout bag as well."

He walks past me, his arm brushing mine ever so slightly. The scent of him invades and assaults my senses. I feel somewhat dazed and wobbly. Like a new foal trying to find its legs.

Maybe that's why I hear myself saying, "Jack?"

He turns back. "Yeah?"

"I, uh … I don't need a takeout cup or bag."

A slow smile spreads across his face. A dimple appearing in his cheek that I didn't notice before. "Okay."

I take a seat on the chair I was holding on to, making sure not to look at Jack across the coffee shop.

He returns five minutes later with our coffees and my bagel.

"Thanks," I say to him when he puts my food and drink in front of me. "How much do I owe you?"

"It's on me."

"You sure?" I check.

"I'm sure. I still owe you for looking out for Eleven."

"Like I said before, I didn't mind. She's a friendly kitty. How is she, by the way? She made any more escape attempts?" I ask because I haven't seen her in a while so I'm assuming she's stayed put.

"Nope. She's decided to take a break from escaping the apartment."

I laugh, picking my coffee up and taking a sip. "Has she always been an escape artist?" I ask him.

He shrugs. "I wouldn't know. I only got her recently. I had just come back to the States, and I found her wandering down the side of the freeway. She's lucky she didn't get killed. Anyway, I pulled my bike over, and she came to me, no problem. Practically leaped into my arms. She was scared witless. I took her to the local vet, and she wasn't microchipped. They thought that she had been dumped by her owner. So, it was either she stayed with me or went to a shelter. There was never any question that I wouldn't take her home to live with me." He shrugs, taking a sip of his own coffee.

She was dumped? And he rescued her.

Sweet Jesus.

An unexpected lump appears in my throat. "I hate people sometimes. Well, most of the time," I say. "Humans really don't deserve animals."

He's watching me with those sharp, knowing eyes of his, and I suddenly feel like I said too much. When, really, I haven't said much at all.

"I would agree with you on that. We don't deserve animals. But I wouldn't say I hate people. There are some shitty ones. But overall, most people are good."

I say nothing. Because I don't have anything to add.

I pick at my bagel, putting a piece in my mouth. "So, you said you came back to the States recently. Had you lived abroad?"

I don't know why I'm asking questions and being this nosy; it is out of the norm for me. When I ask questions, they usually get asked back, so I don't put myself in that situation. But something about Jack has me intrigued.

"I had just come back from Syria. I was in the military. It was my last tour."

"Oh, wow. Well, thank you for your service." The words immediately bounce back at me, and I cringe. "Was that as patronizing as it sounded in my head?"

He laughs. "No. And my service was my pleasure."

The smile on his lips and the look in his eyes make those words sound a whole lot less clean than he said them, and it makes me feel flustered. And hot.

I take another sip of my coffee.

"So, you're out of the military. What are you doing now? Aside from sitting around in libraries and coffee shops." I smile so that he knows I am teasing.

"Writing. I'm an author. I've been doing it for years, even while I was still in the military."

He's an author. Makes sense why he was spending so much time in the library. Probably doing research for his next book.

"Wow. A real-life author."

I see a slight blush on the tops of his cheekbones. I find myself thinking it's adorable, and then I want to slap myself.

And I also might work in a library, but I have never actually met an author. Well, not that I know of. It's not like I actively try to get to know people. Avoiding people is my specialty. And yet, here I am, chatting with Jack.

"I'm assuming you're published?"

He nods.

"Would I have heard of you?"

Something dark flashes through his eyes. "Probably not." He lets out a laugh that sounds self-deprecating and out of odds with the expression I just saw in his eyes.

"Hey, I work in a library. I've read a lot of authors. What genre do you write?"

"Crime."

And a chill cuts into the warmth that he unknowingly placed in my chest.

I sit back in my seat, hands curling around my coffee cup. "Crime books aren't my thing. But I might have seen your name while I was filing books away. What's your pen name?"

"Jack Canti."

Jack Canti. Can a name be sexy? Yes. Yes, it can.

"Jack Canti," I echo my thoughts. "So, is Jack Canti your real name or a pseudo name?"

I know that authors who have pseudo names will sometimes use them in real life with people they don't know.

"Real," he answers slowly.

"Then, nope, I haven't heard of you."

I smile, and he laughs.

I find myself loving the sound of it. I like being the one who made him laugh.

"But I am definitely going to look you up when I get back to the library."

"You're on your lunch break right now?" he asks me.

"Yep. And I should be heading back," I say, glancing at the clock on the wall. I've hardly even touched the bagel. I pick it up and quickly finish it off before swigging down the rest of my coffee. "Sorry to rush off," I tell him.

"No problem."

He's watching me with those intense eyes and smiling at me, and it makes me feel flustered again.

"And thanks again for the coffee and bagel," I tell him, getting out of my seat.

He answers by way of a shrug.

"So, I guess I'll see you …" I say, letting the words hang.

I'm hesitating. Stalling leaving. And I don't know why.

Maybe it's because you don't know when you'll see Jack next, whispers my subconscious.

Nope. I might find the guy hot, but I'm not hanging out, waiting to hear when I will see him next.

I don't do people. I don't do friends.

Yet isn't that what Jack is to me now … a friend?

Ugh.

I really need to get out of here. Now.

"So, yeah … bye."

"See you tomorrow, Audrey," he says, his words catching my back, turning me around again.

"Tomorrow?" I question.

A smile lifts his eyes. "At the library." He says this like I should have already known the answer.

And I hate that my heart is doing a happy dance in my chest right now.

So, I conceal my feelings and act casual and shrug. "Sure. See you tomorrow."

And I turn and walk out of the coffee shop, unable to keep the smile off my face, thanking God that Jack can't see it.

NINE

"Thanks." I pay the cab driver, exiting the car.

Palming the building's security fob and my apartment keys in one hand, my rape alarm in the other, I walk quickly toward the entrance to my apartment building, hearing the cab drive away behind me.

I don't usually like to take cabs. Getting in a car with someone I don't know is not exactly my favorite thing to do.

But it was either that or walk home in the dark.

I ended up working late, covering for a member of the staff who had called in sick today and monitoring a book club that met tonight at the library. So, I said that I would stay while they were there and locked up after they left.

Hence the cab ride home.

And at least a cab driver is registered. So, if I were killed, there would be a good chance of catching him.

If I walked home and got grabbed, severely less chance of catching the killer.

I know; I'd end up dead in both of those scenarios, which wouldn't be good for me, obviously. But I've escaped death at the hands of a psychopath before. I don't think I can do it twice. Don't get me wrong; I would put up one hell of a fight, but I don't see myself being so lucky twice.

Which is why I'm not keen on ending up in a situation like that ever again.

I didn't fight back when Tobias had me … and I hate that so much. I hate that I was frozen there with terror and did nothing to try and save my own life.

I was tied up, so it wasn't like I could have done much. But I did nothing.

I didn't even try.

The only reason I lived was because he let me.

But I won't make that mistake again. That, I know for sure.

I swipe the fob, letting myself into the building, hearing the door click shut behind me.

The well-lit entry hall is devoid of people.

Not that I usually see many people when I come home at my normal hour. But it's daylight then, and it doesn't seem as eerie as it does right now.

Goose bumps skitter up my arms, moving me forward. I jog up the stairs, my bag bumping against my hip, until I reach my floor.

I fast-walk to my apartment, unlock the door, and let myself inside. It's pitch-black in here. My heart is banging in my chest. I hate the dark. Shutting the door closed, I flick on the light switch. It comes on, followed by a pop, and I'm plunged straight back into darkness.

Shit.

The lightbulb has blown.

I scramble to get my phone out of my bag, somehow dropping my rape alarm and keys at the same time.

"Fuck."

My hand curls around my cell, and I yank it out of my bag. I touch the screen, illuminating it, and turn on the Flashlight app.

Light shines out from my cell. But it's not enough. It hardly illuminates anything.

My breath is coming in quicker. Fear of the dark starting to take over.

Calm down, Audrey.

I shine the flashlight down to the floor to find the things I dropped. I locate my keys and rape alarm. Bending down, I pick them up and pocket them. I put my bag down near the wall by the door.

I need to get the lights back on, but I can't remember where the fuse box is.

Okay, so truth is, I don't actually know where the fuse box is.

I'm not a practical person. I always relied on my dad and then Cole for this kind of thing.

Fucking fuck.

My anxiety is quickly building. I can feel fear and adrenaline starting to pump around my body.

I need to calm down.

I'm fine. It's just a bulb that's blown out. I'm not in any danger.

Deep breath.

I suck in some oxygen and slowly release it.

Right, if I were a fuse box, where would I be?

A cupboard maybe.

Think, Audrey. Do you remember any fuse-looking boxes in any of the cupboards in the kitchen?

Nope. But then would a fuse box even be in the kitchen?

Why don't I know this?

Because you're useless, Audrey.

I can't even argue with myself on that one because it's the truth.

Closet! In my bedroom!

There's a white box up above the shelf where the hanging rail is. That's surely got to be it.

Holding my cell in front of me, shining the light ahead, I start making my way toward my bedroom.

I see *it* the second I step into the hallway.

"Oh fuck. *No.*"

A dead rat. On the floor outside of my bedroom.

No.

My heart bangs hard against my ribs. Tremors run through my body. The hand holding my cell shakes.

My mind flashes to the first time I ever saw a dead animal, my memory dragging me back to a place I never want to go, rooting my feet to the spot.

Swinging open the door, I expect to find another one of those notes that this stranger has been leaving daily for me.

But there is no note.

Only a dead bird.

I didn't know in that moment … I thought it had died of natural causes.

It hadn't.

It was a gift from Tobias. One of his many sick gifts.

It's starting again.

No. No, it's not. This is a rat.

70

DEAD PRETTY

Not a bird or a cat.

A rat.

Calm down.

But I can't seem to.

My pulse is beating wildly.

Rational thoughts only, Audrey.

There are a hundred reasons as to why a dead rat is in my apartment. It could have easily gotten inside.

Rats can do that. They can go anywhere.

Only it's not a small rat. In terms of rat size, it's definitely at the larger end of the scale.

It could have gotten in under the front door. They do that.

Not that I have a big gap under my door.

Maybe a window? It could have crawled in through a window.

Yeah, it shimmied up the drainpipe to the second floor and crawled in through my locked window.

Fear sprints down my spine, spinning me into action. My pulse is beating wildly in my ears.

I whirl around. My cell flies out of my hand.

Shit!

I hear my phone clatter to the floor, but I don't have time to stop and look for it.

I have to get out of here.

I rush through my apartment, heading for the only exit I have—the front door.

There's no outline of light around the door, meaning the lights are out in the hall too.

Breaths are panting out of me. Reaching the door in no time, I grab the handle and yank it open.

And a dark figure is standing there.

TEN

I don't scream.

Instead, I yell, "*Fire!*" at the top of my lungs. Because that always brings people running.

Self-defense class taught me that screaming or calling for help will bring no one. But yell *fire*—actual danger—and people will come running straight toward it.

Then, I clench my fist and punch upward as hard as I can, upper-cutting, hoping to connect with some part of the person's body. But it's dark, and I can't see a goddamn thing.

I hit bone—chin, I think—and pain explodes in my hand.

I hear a grunt of pain and then, "What the fuck, Audrey!"

Jack.

It's Jack. And I just punched him in the face.

"What the hell are you doing, standing outside my front door?" I snap at him. My heart is knocking so hard against my ribs that I expect one of them to break at any moment.

"I knocked!" he exclaims. "I just wanted to check if your lights were out too!"

He knocked on my door?

I must not have heard him when I was too busy freaking out over the rat.

The big, dead rat that's still in my apartment.

Fuck.

"We have to get out of here." I try to shove him backward, so I can get past him, but he's not budging.

Two strong hands curl around my upper arms, gripping them, stopping me. "Audrey, what the hell is going on?" His voice is gentle but firm.

"There's—" I cut off, my jaw clenching tightly shut. Because what am I going to say? *There's a deceased rat in my apartment, and because of that, I think someone is here to kill me?*

If Jack doesn't already think I'm crazy, he most definitely would if I said that.

"Nothing. Nothing's going on. You just startled me."

"Audrey, you just screamed *fire*, punched me in the face, and then told me that *we have to get out of here*, so when you say nothing is going on, I kinda find that hard to believe. That, and the fact that your whole body is shaking."

I'm shaking?

It takes me a second to realize that he's right. And also that his hands are still holding on to my arms.

I step back out of his grasp and wrap my arms around myself to stave off the trembling in my body. "Well, it's the truth. Nothing is wrong."

There's a brief pause and then a flicker of illumination from a cell phone screen before a bright light in the form of a phone flashlight comes on.

And I see Jack's face for the first time tonight.

The face I just punched.

"So, there isn't a fire?" he says, eyes fixed on mine.

"Nope."

"Why did you say there was?"

"Because … you startled me. I thought maybe you were a robber, and the best way to get people's attention to come and help is to yell *fire*."

Although I am just realizing that no one came running to my aid.

Guess my neighbors don't give a shit about a fire burning the building down.

I am also still consciously aware of the dead rat and the fact that a psycho killer could be lurking somewhere close by.

I hold off the shudder that wants to make its way through my body.

Jack's eyes briefly leave mine and stare over my shoulder, into the darkness behind me.

"Look, I'm going to go downstairs to the super's place and see what's happening with the lights. Do you want to come with me?"

Do I want to stay in my pitch-black apartment, alone with the dead rat and God knows who else? Or go downstairs with Jack?

"Let's go."

I close my apartment door behind me and walk down the darkened hallway with Jack, using his light to guide the way.

Aside from the nerves flitting around my chest from being in the near dark, that ugly emotion that I hate so much starts to work its way in there too. Guilt.

"Jack?"

"Yep?"

"I'm, uh … sorry that I punched you."

I hear a chuckle and then, "Apology accepted. You got me good though. Pretty sure I'll have a bruise there tomorrow."

"Sorry," I mumble.

"Where did you learn to hit like that?"

"Krav Maga. I took some classes a while back."

"They clearly taught you well. I'm impressed."

We've just reached the stairs when the lights flicker back on, blinding me.

"Jesus." I blink rapidly, trying to adjust to the brightness. I squint up at Jack, who seems to have no trouble adjusting to the light at all.

He smiles at me. "Guess that saves us a trip downstairs."

"I guess so."

We both turn and walk back in the direction of our apartments.

We reach Jack's door first.

"Sorry again." I gesture to his face as he opens his door.

He smiles again. "Don't worry about it. It's not the first time I've been punched. Won't be the last."

I laugh softly. "Night, Jack."

I walk the short distance to my door. Remembering exactly what is waiting for me inside it.

My anxiety ramps up.

DEAD PRETTY

It's just a dead rat. It doesn't mean anything bad is going to happen. I have to go back in my apartment at some point.

It's not like I can stay out here all night.

I'll just carry my rape alarm with me while I do my usual apartment check. And dispose of the rat.

I reach my door.

I didn't lock it.

I never forget to lock it.

But then it wasn't exactly a normal situation.

There's already a dead rat in there. It can't get any worse.

Okay, it can get worse. Like a psycho could be waiting for me in there.

But I try not to freak myself out.

I take a fortifying breath and swing open the door.

My apartment is still pitch-black. Because I didn't get a chance to turn any lights on.

I reach my hand out, searching for the light switch on the wall. Finding it, I flick it on. But nothing happens.

And that's because your lightbulb blew out, dumbass.

I don't have a spare one in the apartment to replace it with either.

Double, triple, and quadruple fuck.

I can't spend the whole night with the living room in darkness. I just can't.

What am I going to do?

I could ask Jack if he has a spare bulb I could borrow.

On a sigh, I lock the door behind me, walk over to Jack's place, lift a hand, and knock on his door.

The door swings open a few moments later.

"Hey." I give him an awkward smile. "You, uh, don't happen to have a spare lightbulb I could borrow, do you?"

"Yours blown?"

"Yep."

"I'm guessing we all have the same fittings, so, yeah, sure, give me a sec." He goes back inside his apartment, leaving the door open and me in the hallway.

I lean into the doorway. "I appreciate this," I tell him. "I'll go to the store first thing tomorrow morning and get you one to replace it."

"No need." He appears back in the doorway. "Do you have a stepladder?"

I give him a confused look. "No. Why?"

His eyes drag up and down the length of me, and I forget to breathe for a moment. My pulse quickens, and I suddenly feel a lot warmer than I did a second ago.

His eyes finally come back to mine. They look a lot darker than they did. "Well …" The word comes out croaky. He clears his throat. "Unless you can grow a good few feet in the next minute or so, you're going to need one to reach the light fitting."

"Ah. Right. Yeah." My cheeks are hot with embarrassment—and also the stupid attraction I have to this guy.

"Don't worry. I've got one."

He disappears again, giving my face and body a moment to cool down before he's back again with a stepladder in his other hand.

"Do you want me to replace the lightbulb for you?" he asks.

He thinks I'm useless. He wouldn't be wrong.

"No. I've got it." I reach out to take the stepladder and bulb from him. "I'll bring the ladder back when I'm done."

"Who's going to hold the flashlight for you?" he questions.

"What?"

"Flashlight," he repeats, his arms folding across his broad chest.

I wonder if his chest is smooth or has hair. I hope it has some hair.

I hate smooth chests on men.

Christ almighty. It's not like I'm ever going to see his chest, so I don't need to be thinking about it.

"Why would I need someone to hold a flashlight for me? I've got a bulb right here to fix my light problem." I lift said bulb up.

He grins. His lips lifting at one corner, showing that dimple.

I have the urge to press my finger into it.

I really need to stop with the sexy thoughts.

"So you can see to fit the lightbulb. I'm guessing your living room is in darkness. Wouldn't want you falling off that ladder."

Duh. Of course. I'm such a dumbass at times.

Instead of letting my idiocy or embarrassment get the better of me again, I grin and say, "You are, soldier. So, bring your phone. Unless you have a flashlight, of course. You seem to have everything else."

Another grin. "Ex-soldier. I'm a civilian now, remember? And actually, no, I don't have a flashlight."

"I'm shocked." I give a mock-surprised look.

He shakes his head at me, but he's smiling. "I lost my old one. Been meaning to buy a new one."

"Slacker."

"Says the woman without a lightbulb."

"Yeah. But I wasn't a soldier. I have no concept of needing to be prepared."

"Everyone should be prepared. And do you really know how to change a lightbulb? Or should I expect another blackout?"

"Hilarious." I roll my eyes.

He chuckles. "Come on, rookie. Let's get your lightbulb changed."

He reaches out and takes the stepladder and bulb from my hands to carry them for me.

I don't argue. I let him do the gentlemanly thing.

We walk in silence to my apartment.

And in those moments, all I can think is … *Were we actually flirting just then?*

How bad is it that I have no clue? I'm that out of practice.

Not that I'm practicing anything with Jack. No matter how much my libido would like me to.

I know Jack's attracted to me. The fact that he asked me out last week clued me in on that one. And I'm definitely attracted to him.

But nothing is ever going to happen between us.

Just being friendly with him is breaking my own rules.

We reach my door, and I hesitate.

If Jack notices, he doesn't say.

Forcing my arm to move, I get my key from my pocket and unlock the door.

As expected, it's still pitch-black inside my apartment. Light from the hall illuminates the entryway.

Jack turns on the Flashlight app on his cell and shines it into my apartment.

"Leave the door open to give us a little extra light," Jack says, and I nod in answer and leave it wide open.

I go inside first, Jack following behind.

Jack sets the stepladder below the light fixture. "You sure you don't want me to replace the bulb for you?" he checks.

I look up at the light, and it seems a lot higher than I first realized. But I made a whole deal out of being able to do it. So, I sigh and say, "No, it's fine. But thanks."

Jack shines the flashlight upward for me as I make my way up the steps. I reach up to remove the broken lightbulb. I get it out and hand it to Jack, and then I insert the new one.

I did it. See, I'm not totally useless.

"Done?" Jack asks.

"Yep." I smile to myself.

He holds out a hand to help me back down the steps, shining the flashlight so I can see my way.

I slide my hand in his. Heat sizzles up my arm. His palm is rough and warm, and his hand dwarfs mine.

I have a flash of visions of what it would be like to have his hands all over my body.

Jesus.

I wish I could turn my attraction to him off. I have always been able to control everything in my life. Every emotion and feeling, I just shut it off. But this ever-growing attraction to Jack … it won't seem to go away. I can see now that the only way to make it disappear is to not see him anymore.

But since he lives on the same floor as me and comes into my place of work on a regular basis, I don't see how it's possible. Unless I quit my job and move.

Which seems quite a drastic thing to do to squash my attraction to him.

Nope. I'm just going to have to woman up and get past it.

"Thanks," I say to him through a mouth of cotton when my foot hits the floor of my living room.

But I don't remove my hand from his. And he doesn't let go either.

Remove your hand, Audrey, my brain issues the command.

My body just isn't complying.

I'm too focused on the feel of his hand in mine.

He moves his finger over the soft skin on the inside of my wrist.

My body's reaction is strong; my breath hitches, and there's a tug in my belly.

So much for womaning up and getting past my attraction to him.

He slides his cell into his pocket, muting the light, and his free hand finds my hip. Fingers curling around it.

My hands land on his biceps. "Jack." His name comes out in a breathy whisper.

My heart is pounding. It's so loud that I'm sure he can hear it.

He's going to kiss me.

And I'm going to let him.

I really shouldn't. But I can't seem to remember the reasons why I should stop what's about to happen.

A door bangs from somewhere in the hallway, and I jerk out of Jack's hold.

It's the wake-up call I needed.

What the hell am I doing? I make rules for myself, and the minute a hot guy comes along, I throw them all out the window.

I march over to the wall and flick the switch on, lighting up the whole room.

Jack blinks over at me. He has a look on his face that I can't fully decipher. But it looks like surprise.

I'm assuming it's because I broke whatever moment was about to happen between us.

"Audrey …" His voice is dark and smoky, and I know he's going to say something that I don't want to hear.

"Thanks for coming over to help me," I say in a clear, steady voice.

He stares at me for a beat.

Just let it go, I silently plead.

He seems to come to some decision in his mind. He nods and says, "No problem." He folds up the stepladder.

"I'll replace your bulb tomorrow," I say, needing to fill the tension-fueled air.

"Audrey, it's not a problem."

"No, I'll replace it." I'm firm with my words. I hate owing people anything.

He nods again, accepting.

Then, he moves toward me, passing by the bedroom hallway, and I know the exact moment that he spots the dead rat because he stops still and stares over at it.

Shit!

How the hell did I forget about it?

Um … because your brain was overrun by your stupid sex hormones.

"Audrey"—he turns to look at me—"did you know there's a dead rat in your apartment?"

Yes. No.

Shit.

Do I tell him that I knew? Or do I play dumb?

Won't he wonder why I didn't say something to him before?

Oh, Jack, by the way, there's a dead rat lying on my hallway floor.

"No." The lie is out of my mouth before I even truly knew I was going to say it. "Where is it?" I ask, trying to sound as innocent as possible. I walk over to where he is, stopping when the rat comes into my view. It's even bigger than I first thought. "Oh God," I say, feigning surprise.

"I take it, it wasn't a pet?" he jokes before he walks over to the rat, leaning the stepladder against the wall.

But I'm really not in the mood for joking right now. I just wish he would leave, so I could get rid of the dead animal and put this whole shitty night behind me.

"No," I answer, following behind him.

"It's a big fucker," he comments, crouching down beside it. "Looks like it broke its neck."

"Maybe it fell," I offer up.

Jack's eyes lift to the solid plasterboard ceiling above our heads.

"Or not," I add quietly.

"Weird that it broke its neck," he muses.

He's right. It is weird. Rats' necks just don't break of their own accord.

Shit. Shit. Shit.

Someone killed it. They wrung that poor rat's neck and left it here for me to find.

No. Stop it. Calm down.

There is a rational explanation as to how that rat ended up in my apartment with a broken neck.

There has to be.

But truthfully, I'm not feeling confident in that theory.

What I am is scared and stressed and confused.

"And you didn't put a rat trap down or anything?" Jack asks, unaware of my internal anguish.

"No!" I snap, my anger and fear flying out of me and heading straight toward Jack. "I fucking told you that I didn't know the damn rat was even here!"

Jack pauses, his sharp eyes trained straight on me.

Shit.

I can feel my cheeks heat with guilt and shame. I move my eyes away from his, which is damn easy to do this time. "Look ... I'm sorry I snapped. I'm just ..." I thrust a hand through my hair. All I ever seem to be doing around Jack is apologizing. "I really appreciate you helping me out. But I'm tired and cranky. I've had a long day, and I just need to get some sleep."

"Okay," he says in a low voice. "Do you need me to help dispose of the rat before I go?" he asks.

He's still being kind to me after I just bit his head off. Not to mention the fact that I punched the guy in the face earlier.

God, I'm a terrible person.

Sighing at myself, I lift my eyes to look at him. I shake my head. "But I appreciate the offer all the same. And thanks again for the bulb."

I start to move toward the front door. Jack grabs his ladder and follows me.

He stops in the hallway and turns back to me. He gives me an uneasy smile. "See you later, Audrey."

I should just let him go. Let my bad behavior put him off me.

But I say his name before I can even stop myself.

I let out a breath. I know that apologizing to him—again—is only going to keep us being friends, but I do it all the same because I'm an idiot. And a slave to my hormones.

"I know I hit you earlier"—I wince because it sounds so awful to say—"but in my defense, it was self-defense." I shrug. "And I also just bit your head off for no good reason, but … I'm not a bad person. Really. I'm just … out of practice … with people."

Stop talking, Audrey. Stop now.

He puts the stepladder on the floor, keeping hold of it in his hand. "Should I even ask why you're out of practice with people?"

I shake my head, and he chuckles, which makes me smile.

"I'll bring that bulb by tomorrow," I tell him, my hand on the door. "And don't tell me not to bother," I add when he parts his lips to speak.

"Wasn't going to." He gives me a grin that makes my stomach flip like a pancake. "You bringing that bulb by tomorrow just means that I'll get to see you again."

Then, that grin widens into a knee-buckling, eye-dazzling smile, and my stomach drags my ovaries into happy backflips with it.

"See ya," he murmurs, that grin still in his voice. Then, he walks off toward his apartment, leaving me standing there like the fool I am.

I let out a breath and then shut my apartment door behind me, locking it up.

DEAD PRETTY

I head into my kitchen and grab rubber gloves, a trash bag, and some paper towels, so I can get this rat out of here, and after that, I'm gonna check every nook and cranny of my apartment, making sure nothing or no one else is lurking here.

And when that's all done, I'll Google large rats and look up how easy it is for them to get inside a second-floor apartment and also how likely it is for one to break its neck without falling or any outside help.

Although I already have a feeling that I know the answer to both of those questions.

ELEVEN

It's just after lunch. I went into town to pick up a lightbulb for Jack. I'm heading home now to give it to him. I have a feeling of nervous energy inside of me at the thought of seeing him. I hope he's home and not out somewhere, writing. Well, if he is out, I'll just wait and give it to him later.

I can feel the disappointment running through me at the mere thought.

I don't want to wait to see him.

And that in itself is dangerous to me.

I'm starting to get attached to him, and I can't.

So, I won't drop by his apartment straightaway. I'll wait and give it to him later. Maybe even tomorrow.

Oh, who am I kidding? I'll—

My thoughts are stopped in their tracks at the sight of a crowd of people and police cars outside my apartment building.

Jack.

My legs pick up speed, quickly bringing me closer. Well, as quick as one can go in the snow. The plastic bag in my gloved hand bangs against my thigh as I move.

What if something's happened to him?

Don't panic. It could be anything. And a lot of people live in my building. It might not be Jack.

As I near, I see it's not my building. It's the apartment building next to mine.

Thank God.

My heart rate evens out now that I know it's not Jack. That he's okay.

But I can't even start to assess my reaction to this. Thinking it was him. And how that made me feel.

I reach the crowd of people, coming to a stop.

This scene isn't something I like or even want to be around. It reminds me too much of my past. But I'm compelled to stay for some reason.

"Girl's been murdered," a voice says next to me.

I turn my head to the person. A woman with a grandmotherly face and grayish tint to her faded brown hair is looking back at me. She's bundled up like I am in a thick brown wool coat and a knit scarf.

"Found her dead this morning. I didn't know her well. She lived in the apartment above me. Sarah, she was called. Always smiled and said hello."

I'm staring at her mouth, trying to take in the words coming from them. Her teeth are crooked and have a slight yellowing to them that comes only from smoking.

"It's scary, something like this happening on your own doorstep. You just don't expect it, do you?"

She puts one of those e-cigarettes in her mouth and starts to puff on it. "Had to give up the smokes." She gestures to the e-cigarette like I asked her a question. "Doctor's orders."

"Do ... did ... they say what happened to the girl?"

She takes another puff of her e-cigarette and shrugs. "Just know that the super found her this morning. Blood everywhere, he said. It's shocked the hell out of him, and that man is as tough as they come. Was in the military. Went to 'Nam. Seen it all. But said he had seen nothing like this."

"Blood everywhere."

My vision starts to go hazy.

Another girl dead.

"Such a shame," she continues. "A real waste. Pretty girl she was."

"What did she look like?" The words shoot out of me like bullets.

A flash of surprise covers the woman's face. Probably from my hard tone.

She shrugs again. "Blonde. Pretty. Kinda like you."

"Kinda like you."

I feel winded.

No. It can't be right.

"You're sure she looked like me?"

She frowns. Her set lines creasing deeper. "You okay, honey? You look a little pale. Did you know Sarah?"

"No." I shake my head, taking a step backward. "I just …" *You just what? Make something up, so you don't sound crazy.* "It's just … worrisome. A murder happening so close by."

She nods, puffing on that e-cigarette. It smells like candy. It's making me feel sick.

"You live round here?"

"Next building," I tell her.

She nods. "Well, I wouldn't worry, hon. I imagine it was her boyfriend. Usually is when things like this happen."

"She had a boyfriend?"

"Yeah. I saw her with him every now and then."

A weird feeling of relief passes through me. I mean, she had a boyfriend, and most murders happen at the hand of those you know and love. It's only rare occasions when people are murdered by strangers. Even rarer when a stranger kills because of an obsession with you.

I need to stop jumping to the worst conclusion. This has nothing to do with Tobias.

This girl was most likely killed by her boyfriend. It's horrific and tragic, and I hope the guy rots in prison. But it is nothing for me to panic over.

"I always thought they were a funny couple though. She was real friendly. Would always smile, say hello. He was weird, I thought. Just this vibe about him. He wouldn't ever talk. Would look right through you, like you weren't even there." She shudders. "Probably should have seen it coming. It's always the quiet ones, right?"

I nod, agreeing with the old adage. Not that it's right. Sometimes but not always. Psychos can also blend right in with the rest of us.

I catch sight of movement by the entry door to the building. I rise onto my tiptoes, so I can see over the heads in front of me. Police are coming out.

Then, it hits me. I'm just like those people who used to stand over Tobias's victims. Vultures waiting to pick at the bones of the story. Like the people who used to wait around outside my old home to get a look at the woman who had caused the death of multiple innocent women. Gossipers like the woman beside me.

This isn't me. I shouldn't be here.

"I have to go," I feel the need to tell this woman, already moving away.

"Stay safe, hon," she says.

I nod and turn away, making my way through the crowd of people, which has grown in size since I got here.

I walk toward my building, a heaviness settling on me.

Another life snuffed out too early.

God, I really hate people at times.

The door to my building opens just as I reach it.

"Jack." A rush of feelings overwhelms me at the sight of him. A sudden urge to put myself in his arms and have him hold me is strong.

I have to press my feet to the ground to stop myself from giving in to the urge.

"Hey." His breath fogs in the cold. He moves his eyes to the side, looking at the crowd I just left. "What's going on over there?"

I stare at him a moment before I answer, "A woman was murdered. The super of the building found her in her apartment."

I watch as any expression disappears from his face, smoothing out. His eyes are fixed on the crowd ahead.

It seems like a long time, but it's probably only seconds before he does anything. And it comes in the form of a blink. Then, his face moves back into an easy expression, the one I know him for.

He turns his eyes back to mine. "Do you know what happened?"

I don't know what I expected him to say, but it wasn't that. "No."

His eyes move down to the bag in my hand. "You been shopping?" he asks.

I'm jolted by the abrupt subject change.

"Er … yeah. I just went to buy the lightbulb I owe you." I hold the bag, containing said lightbulb, out to him.

He takes it from me. "Thanks."

"Thanks for the loan and the help last night."

He shrugs.

There's a moment of silence between us. It's almost … awkward.

Like we used to have in the beginning when I first met him.

I feel compelled to fill it.

"Are you going out?" I ask him.

"What? Oh, yeah." He glances back at the door behind him. "I'm just … going for a walk."

In the snow? Although I guess it's all we have weather-wise around here, so if he wants to take a walk, he doesn't have much of a choice.

I look down at his clothes.

He's in his usual garb of jeans, T-shirt, leather jacket, and motorcycle boots.

"You might want to reconsider putting on at least a hat or scarf. It's piss cold out here if you haven't noticed."

I expect him to chuckle or, in the very least, smile, but he doesn't.

Then again, a girl has just been found dead. Laughter of any kind would be really inappropriate.

"The cold doesn't bother me."

I should have guessed that about him. It's not like I ever see him wearing anything other than what he has on.

"Okay. Well, have a nice walk." I don't want to end my time with him, but I feel like I should.

The air between us seems different. Uncomfortable almost. Nothing like it was last night.

If I didn't know better, I would think that I did something wrong.

But I did do something wrong last night. Punched him—which was by accident, kind of—and was an ass to him. I apologized, which he accepted at the time, but maybe he's changed his mind.

"Jack … is everything okay?"

He gives me a confused look, brows pulling together. "Why wouldn't it be?"

"You just seem … never mind. Enjoy your walk."

I move past him, walking toward the door to take me into our apartment building.

"Stay safe," Jack says to me.

His words and low tone make me pause and turn back. But Jack is already striding away, heading in the direction I just came from.

I let myself inside the building, heading up to my apartment.

It's not until later, when I'm sitting on my sofa with my latest book and a cup of coffee, that I realize it.

It's a small thing. But it's been there, niggling on the fringes of my consciousness.

Jack didn't smile when he first saw me.

I know it sounds stupid. But Jack always smiles at me.

Always. I noticed because I liked it.

And today, he didn't.

The day a woman is found murdered.

Also, now that I think about it … he didn't seem shocked or surprised when I told him about the murder.

It was almost like he'd already known it happened.

TWELVE

I take the young girl's library card from her and begin checking out the stack of books she brought to the desk.

Some good books in here, I muse as I scan the label on each one, creating a new pile of books to go.

I'm working on the checkout desk.

I don't usually work here. I prefer not to. Facing people isn't my thing. But we're a staff member short today.

Mike didn't show up for work, which isn't like him. Well, that's what our manager, Margaret, told me.

She said she called him, and he didn't answer. She seems concerned. He's probably just sick, and that's why he isn't answering.

I told her not to worry.

Mike's worked here longer than me. He's quiet, like me. Keeps to himself.

Honestly, I don't know him that well.

I hardly know anyone in this town.

Except for Jack.

Jack, who has been on my mind since yesterday.

Well, mainly, his reaction has been bothering me—or lack of a reaction to a woman being murdered in the building next to ours.

But I guess not everyone reacts the same, and it's not like he knew the woman. Also, Jack must have seen a lot of death, being in the military.

That has to be it. There's no way he already knew because he wouldn't have asked me what was happening if he did.

And if he did know, then it would have been because he …

Nope. Not Jack.

I'm not that unlucky.

Right?

I place the last book on the pile. "All done," I tell her.

The girl picks up the books and puts them in the canvas bag she's carrying. "Thanks." She gives me a smile.

I smile back. "Have a good day," I tell her.

Look at me, being all pleasant.

Not that I would ever be an asshole to a kid.

I'm a lot of things, but I would never upset a child. Even I have my limits to my bitchiness.

Folding my arms on the counter, I rest against it, looking around the quiet place. People reading. Students working. Some on laptops, tapping away.

But no Jack.

I didn't see him again after our run-in yesterday. Part of me had thought he might come to see me. Okay, I'd hoped he would come see me. But he didn't.

Ugh. Why does everything in my brain automatically take me to Jack?

Because you're seriously into him.

I don't even get to process that thought further because the library doors open, bringing in two policemen.

Both in plain clothes.

How do I know they're police?

Because I have spent enough time around the police to recognize them when I see them.

I watch them approach.

The taller of the two men is in his early thirties, I would say. Red hair, cut short. Smart suit. Clean-cut look to him. Handsome too. The other guy is older. Late forties, early fifties. Dark hair, peppered with gray, which looks like it hasn't seen scissors in a while. Overgrown stubble on his face. Wrinkled suit.

They're a stark contrast.

I straighten up as they come closer, trying to relax but failing.

As much as I respect the police and the job they do, I really don't like seeing them. Especially not when a woman was discovered murdered yesterday.

God, what if they're here to see me? My past might have brought them here.

But why would it? People don't know who I am.

But they're the police. Their job is to know who people are.

But why would they want to see me over the woman who was murdered yesterday? Because you're linked to a serial killer.

And two other women have been murdered since I moved here. Fuck.

The hairs on the nape of my neck rise. I swallow past my nerves.

"Officers," I greet them with a forced smile.

The older of the two smiles back at me, and it's not a smile that puts me at ease.

"I'm Detective Sparks," he tells me. "This is Detective Peters." He gestures to his partner. "We're hoping you can help us."

I swallow again. "With?"

Detective Sparks leans an arm on the desk. "We're looking for someone who works here."

Shit. Shit. Shit.

My hands come together in front of me, fingers gripping together to stop them from trembling. "Wh-who?"

"A … Mr. Michael King."

They're here for Mike?

Relief seeps through me, relaxing me a touch. But not much. If the police are here for Mike, then it's not for a good reason.

"Um, Mike's not here. He didn't show up for work today," I tell them both.

"Have you heard from him at all today?" Detective Peters asks, speaking for the first time.

"No. He didn't call in. Our manager, Margaret, tried calling his cell, but he didn't answer."

"Is your manager still here?" Detective Sparks asks.

"Yes."

"Could you get her for us, please?" Detective Sparks says.

"Um, sure. One minute."

I leave the main desk and walk through the back to Margaret's office.

Her door's open, like it always is.

I stop in the doorway. "Margaret, the police are here."

Her surprised eyes lift to mine over her computer screen.

"The police?" She pushes her seat back, rising to stand.

"Yeah. They're asking about Mike. I told them that he didn't show up today and that you called him but got no answer. They asked me to come get you."

"Oh gosh. Yes, I'm coming now." She rounds the desk.

I step back out of the doorway, allowing her through, and then I follow her back to the main desk, where Detective Sparks and Detective Peters are still waiting.

"Officers ..." Margaret says, holding her hand out to shake theirs.

I stand just off to the side. Not too far away that I can't hear their conversation, but enough that I'm no longer a part of it.

After their brief introductions are done, Margaret says, "You're looking for Mike?"

"Yes," Detective Sparks says. "We need to speak to him urgently. We're told he's not answering his cell?"

"That's correct. I called this morning when he didn't turn up for his shift. It's not like Mike. In the two years he's worked here, he's always been on time. Never had a day off. So, it seemed odd that he hadn't called. I left him a voice mail, asking him to call me back, but I still haven't heard anything. I was going to go to his house later to check on him."

"Speaking of his home, can I confirm his address with you?" Detective Peters says to Margaret.

"Of course."

He hands Margaret a slip of paper.

"Yes, that's Mike's address," she says, reading it before handing it back.

The detectives share a look that I can't decipher.

"Can I ask what this is concerning? Is Mike okay?"

"It's a police matter," Detective Sparks answers curtly. "But the moment you hear from Mike, I want you to call the station immediately." He takes a card from his pocket and places it on the desktop. "This is a central number, but ask for either myself or Detective Peters, and you'll be put straight through to us."

Margaret picks up the card, holding it to her chest. "Okay."

"The moment you hear from him," he emphasizes as though Margaret didn't get the importance the first time.

"Thanks for your time," Detective Peters says.

They both turn to leave, but then Detective Sparks stops and turns back. His eyes finding mine.

"I didn't catch your name, Miss ..." He steps back toward me.

Something in his tone makes my stomach turn over.

I swallow down. "Hayes. Audrey Hayes."

He nods, as though he expected me to say that name all along. "A question, Miss Hayes ... how did you know we were police officers?"

My eyes go to Detective Peters, who is standing where he stopped, and then back to Detective Sparks. I notice how dark and scarily intense his eyes are. "I'm sorry?" I respond, a little confused.

He smiles that awful smile again, a bemused look on his face. "When we first arrived, you greeted us by saying *officers*. Neither of us is uniformed or wearing badges." He shrugs. "Curious, I'm just wondering how you knew we were police."

He's trying to put the question off as nothing. Just mere curiosity. But I know better.

I swallow again. It's a nervous tell, but I can't stop myself from doing it.

I shrug and smile the best I can. "A lucky guess."

Detective Sparks stares at me a moment. "Most people would say it's unlucky when we come calling." He taps his fingers on the wooden desktop with finality. "Have a good day, Miss Hayes."

And then they're both gone, and I let out a breath that feels like it was trapped in my lungs for hours.

THIRTEEN

I've been distracted all day. Ever since that visit from the police and that detective's parting words to me. He knows I have a past with the police, all because of my stupidity.

It will undoubtedly make him curious about me. And when he looks into my name and comes up dry, that will make him even more curious.

Because Hayes was my first surname. Before it was changed to Irwin when I was adopted.

When I moved here, I just went back to my old surname.

Audrey Irwin was the name that was in the news for months.

It was the name linked to the killings.

But it won't be hard for a police officer to trace Audrey Hayes to Audrey Irwin.

Fucking. Fuck.

And even worse, Margaret shared information with me that she'd discovered not long after the police left—that Sarah Greenwood, the woman who had been murdered, was Mike's girlfriend.

And now, he's missing.

The assumption is that he killed her and is now on the run. But Margaret finds it hard to believe. She said Mike isn't a killer. I don't know the guy well enough to form an opinion.

The one thing I do know is, it's always hard for people to accept that someone they know and care about are not who they thought them to be.

I know that Tobias's family, to this day, believes that he's innocent. Even with all the physical evidence against him and after a jury of his peers deemed him to be guilty, they still refuse to accept it.

I've learned from my experiences that nothing is ever as it really seems.

People only allow you to see what they want you to.

You never really know anyone. No matter what you think.

The closest person to you could be hiding all kinds of things.

So, it would be no surprise to me if Mike did murder his girlfriend.

The one thing for me is that Sarah's murder is not connected to the other two unsolved murders, meaning there is no copycat killer in this town.

I do have to wonder what it is about me that seems to attract murderers. I left town to get away from one murderer, only to start working at a job with another murderer.

I don't believe in coincidences. Maybe you could call it bad luck, but I wasn't his victim.

Maybe there are just more evil people in this world than I thought.

After my shift was finished, I helped Margaret close up the library.

She was really distressed by everything going on. So much so that she insisted on driving me home. She said that I shouldn't be walking the streets alone. Not with what had happened.

She might find it hard to think that Mike killed his girlfriend, but regardless, a girl is dead, and a killer is out there somewhere.

If only she knew my past, she would know that walking home alone in daylight was the very least of my fears.

After being dropped off at my apartment building, with a vigilant Margaret waiting until I was inside the building before driving away, I headed up to my apartment and found Eleven waiting outside my door for me.

I was happy to see her, and also, it gave me a reason to knock on Jack's door.

Yes, I am that pathetic.

And I won't lie when I say that I was disappointed when he didn't answer.

I taped a note to his door, letting him know that Eleven was with me. Then, I took a long shower, washing the day off me. Dressed in sweats. Brushed my hair, leaving it to dry naturally. Then, I made dinner for myself and Eleven. She had tuna, and I had a bowl of tomato soup.

I'm curled up on the sofa with Eleven when there's a knock at my door.

"That'll be your dad," I say to Eleven.

Leaving her on the sofa, I go to the door, checking the peephole to ensure that I am right and that it is Jack. I unlock the door and open it to him.

His hair is mussed up. The way it is when he's just taken off his motorcycle helmet.

"Hey."

He smiles at me, and my heart shimmies in my chest.

Stupid heart.

"Hey. Come in. I'll get her for you."

Jack steps inside the doorway, closing the door behind him.

"She's escaping again?" I say to him as I walk over to get Eleven.

"Yep. Still not figured out how she's getting out. Not sure I ever will." He chuckles.

I feel his laughter run down my back like a caress of warm hands.

"How was your day?" he asks me as I pick up Eleven.

I turn back to him, cuddling her to my chest. "Weird," I answer him honestly.

"Weird how?"

"The police came to my work today."

I watch carefully for his reaction. I'm not fully sure why I do this. Maybe it's the untrusting part of me that does.

"The police?"

He's leaning back against the wall. The only expression on his face is the wry lift of his brow. "Someone been stealing books?"

"No. They were looking for a guy who works there. Mike. It was his girlfriend who was found dead yesterday."

I'm still watching.

"No shit," he says.

Still no real facial reaction. His words are not what I would have expected someone to say to that. But then, from everything I have learned, possibly the reaction I expect isn't necessarily the correct one.

Perhaps Jack is reacting as a normal person would. Not a guilty person. Or maybe he's just reacting like Jack would, based on all his life experiences—which I know nothing about. I can only surmise about his time in the military. I know very little about him in general.

But if I got to know him well, then that would mean, in turn, he'd get to know me too. And I can't do that.

"So, what happened? Was the guy there?"

I perch on the edge of my sofa, stroking Eleven, who is still in my arms. "No, he hadn't shown up for work, which is out of character for him. They spoke to my manager, checked his home address with her, and left their number for us to call them if we heard from him. They wouldn't say why they were looking for him. It wasn't until later when my manager heard on the gossip mill that the murdered girl was his girlfriend."

"That's … wow. So, they think he killed her?"

I shrug. "They usually look at the closest people to the deceased, right?"

He nods in response, eyes holding mine.

I look away. "And the fact that he's disappeared isn't helping his case."

"How are you feeling about it?"

My eyes snap back to his. It seems an odd question to ask. "What do you mean?" My words are clipped. If they affect him, he doesn't let on.

Just pushes his hands into his front pockets, rocking on his heels, back still resting against the wall. "I mean, you worked with the guy, and he's potentially a killer. That would weird anyone out, Audrey."

Yes, it would. If I were a normal person who hadn't already experienced the worst of the worst.

"I didn't know him well. We've barely spoken to each other since I started working there. He's like me. Quiet. Doesn't like to talk to people."

Jack stares at me a long moment. "You talk to me."

"Yeah, well …" I look away from his probing gaze, down at Eleven, running my fingers through her soft fur.

"Does that mean that you like to talk to me?"

Eleven jumps down from my lap and wanders into the kitchen. She was the barrier between us, and now, she's left me vulnerable.

Thanks, Eleven.

I curl my toes into the carpet. "Maybe."

A low laugh. I hear him move. Then, he's a shadow on the floor before me. His booted feet a mere inch from mine. I get a whiff of him—leather and cedar. It weakens me way more than it should.

"Audrey." His voice sounds deeper, huskier.

I love hearing him say my name. Just the sound of his voice speaking my name turns me on a ridiculous amount.

I lift my eyes to his.

It's a mistake.

There's fire in his eyes, and it lights one inside of me.

"I like talking to you too," he says.

I wet my lips with my tongue. It's a subconscious move. But one that brings those eyes of his to my mouth.

"God, you're so fucking beautiful."

Shivers send goose bumps racing over my heated skin.

It's not the first time I have had a man say those words to me. I have heard them many times in the past. But coming from Jack, it feels different. It feels like he means *me*. The whole of me. Not just the way I look.

His hand is moving at his side. Fingers shifting restlessly, like they're desperate to touch me. "You know I like you, Audrey. I've made no secret of that fact. The question is … do you like me?"

I do.

I shouldn't, but I do.

I look away from him, trying to sort my tangled thoughts.

"Don't do that." His fingers touch my chin. He gently turns my head, bringing my eyes back to his. "Stay with me."

My heart is beating wildly inside my chest, a feeling of fight-or-flight starting. Both sound like a good option, to be honest.

But because I'm an idiot, I do neither.

I just sit here, staring at him.

"What do you want from me, Jack?" I manage to speak words. The only ones I can come up with. And they sound like a plea.

"Anything. Everything." His eyes flicker down to my lips again. "To know if you taste as good as I think you do."

Holy fuck.

Everything inside of me tightens. *How am I supposed to recover from those words?*

My hands grip the sofa. I'm desperately trying to anchor myself. "We're friends," I croak.

I am trying to fight this. I'm doing a shitty job. But at least I'm trying.

"I thought you didn't have friends," he says, reminding me of my words to him from that day in the supermarket. And he's not being cruel or sarcastic. He's just being Jack. Laying it all out so simply.

I swallow down. "I don't."

His thumb traces a path down my throat, stopping at the hollow of my neck. His fingers curl around my nape.

Adrenaline is running through my body. Making my heart beat faster and my pulse race.

"So, what are we, Audrey?"

"Neighbors?" It sounds like a question.

The light in his eyes dims a little, and he lets out a sound of disappointment.

"Neighbors," he echoes, nodding.

Then, he steps back, his hand leaving my neck.

And I feel cold. Bereft.

I watch him walk over to Eleven and pick her up. Then, he heads straight for the door.

He opens it but glances back at me. "Thanks for watching Eleven, neighbor."

Then, he shuts the door behind him.

And I'm still sitting here, in the exact same spot he left me.

Fuck!

I know this is the right thing. Letting him go. Not letting whatever was about to happen between us happen.

I made my choices a long time ago, and I need to keep sticking with them.

But ...

I could just sleep with him once and then be done.

Yeah, because screwing your neighbor once and then ignoring him is a good idea, said no one ever.

But ...

For fuck's sake!

I'm tired of fighting myself on this. Fighting wanting him.

What's the worst thing that could happen?

I'll get some orgasms, and then we'll never speak again.

Fine!

All rational thought has left me by this point. I'm solely working off emotions right now. A whole fucking mix of them. Want, need, frustration, confusion, and a ton of anger.

I'm angry with myself for being so weak. And I'm pissed at him for making me want him.

Screw it all to hell!

I'm storming out of my apartment and stomping my way over to his before I can even give it another thought.

I bang my fist on his door.

It swings open a few seconds later.

He looks like he's going to say something, but I don't give him a chance to speak.

I hold up my hand, stopping him. "Look, Jack, I don't know what we are, okay!" My voice is starting to rise. I can't seem to stop it. "I have no clue! All I do know is that I want you. I shouldn't, but I do! I want you, and I—" I don't get to finish the rest of that sentence.

Because Jack reaches out, yanks me against his hard body, and kisses the hell out of me.

FOURTEEN

The door is kicked shut. I'm pressed up against a wall.

Jack is kissing me.

Holy shit ... Jack is kissing me.

And I'm letting him.

I shouldn't but—

I part my lips on a breath. His tongue slips into my mouth.

And my brain switches off.

I loop my arms around his neck, holding him close.

He slides his fingers into my hair, gripping the strands, and angles my head exactly where he wants it, so he can kiss me deeper.

It's possessive.

It's raw and needful. Desperate.

And I'm here for all of it.

His thigh slides between mine, parting my legs, bringing our bodies together. I can feel his erection pressed up against my stomach.

Sweet Jesus.

"I was right," he whispers into my mouth.

"About?" I manage to say.

"How good you taste."

I'm pretty sure I moan.

"And you feel even better than anything I could conjure up." His lips are chasing a path down my neck.

"You thought about me? This?"

His eyes come back to mine. "Every fucking night."

He takes my mouth again, the kiss fast becoming desperate again.

My hands slide down his arms, to his waist. Finding the hem of his T-shirt, I slip my hands underneath, against the hard of his back muscles, needing to feel his skin.

Soft. So fucking soft.

I hear a groan.

This time, it's from him.

His erection pushes into my stomach.

I'm panting into his mouth. I feel like I'm going to explode. My clit is throbbing, pressed up against his thigh. I need to move to release the pressure.

As if reading my mind, he starts to move his leg against me, creating a delicious friction against the spot where I need it most.

I feel shameless in this moment.

I'm here, fully dressed, dry-humping my neighbor's leg against his apartment wall, and I don't even care.

I should stop this.

No, you shouldn't. Shut up, Audrey.

That's my vagina talking.

In all honesty, I don't think I could even if I tried.

I want this. I want him.

We're all heat, hands, lips, and tongues.

My hands move to his stomach, feeling the ridges.

Jack breaks our kiss. Reaching his hand to the back of his neck, he grabs hold of his T-shirt and pulls it off over his head in that sexy way that guys do.

He tosses the shirt aside.

My eyes drop lower.

He's cut. My God, is he cut.

My fingers reach out, tracing the lines of his muscles. He has a tattoo on his right bicep.

"Keep looking at me like that, and I will fuck you against this wall."

My eyes lift to his.

The way he's looking at me …

I can't remember any man looking at me with as much heat in his eyes as Jack is right now.

"Alpha much?" I smirk.

So does he.

Then, he kisses me again. Harder. Needier.

I wind my fingers into his hair.

His hand slides slowly up my waist, his thumb grazing the underside of my boob.

Touching yet not touching anywhere nearly enough.

"You want my hands on you?" he murmurs, lips peppering kisses to the side of mine.

"Yes."

His hand covers my breast over my shirt, thumb grazing over my nipple.

"Oh God," I moan.

"He ain't here. But I am."

Jack's hand is on my breast. His thigh moving against my clit. His erection rubbing against my stomach. His tongue back in my mouth.

I'm powerless to resist.

It's been so long. Too long since I've felt like this.

And if I'm being honest, I don't think I have ever felt this good.

"Jack ... I ..."

"Hush, baby. I'll get you there." He sweeps his tongue over my lips, biting down on the bottom one. He kisses across my jaw to my ear. His fingers tweak my nipple. His teeth graze my earlobe. His thigh presses against me.

And I go off like a rocket. Falling apart in his arms.

I can't even think about how vulnerable I am to him right now.

Without a doubt, I would fall to the floor from the force of that orgasm if it wasn't for Jack holding me up.

I'm out of breath, panting.

Jack's lips press soft kisses to my feverish face. "You're so fucking hot when you come."

His mouth comes to mine, kissing me.

I can already feel myself starting to come down from the high he just gave me.

I can also feel the shame coming in. The failure at not even being able to stick to my own stupid rules because of a gorgeous face.

Okay, it's not just his face. I like Jack.

But I'm the way I am for a reason. Getting close to anyone is a bad idea.

I need to get out of here.

"Jack ..."

"Audrey." He rests his forehead to mine, eyes holding me still.

"I ... we ... shouldn't ..."

"Yes, we should."

"I can't ..."

"You like me, Audrey. That much is obvious from the way you came against my leg."

His words are crass. They should offend me. But they don't. Because all they do is make me feel hot.

"And I like you," he continues. "That much is obvious from this." He presses his hard erection against my stomach, making me squirm.

Surely, I can't want more from him already after that spectacular orgasm he just gave me.

His hand lifts to my hair. Brushing it back, he tucks it behind my ear. "So, what's stopping you?"

"I … it's complicated." My eyes slide to the side.

He captures my chin in his palm, bringing my gaze back to his. "Are you married?"

"God, no." I laugh.

"In a relationship?"

"No."

"You like me?"

"Don't seek compliments." I roll my eyes. "You know I do."

"Then, there's nothing complicated about it. Only if you choose to make it so."

I sigh. He doesn't understand. And I can't explain it to him. Because truthfully, sometimes, I don't fully understand it myself.

"I know I'm going ass-backward about this, and this is not the way I intended to do this at all. But let me take you out on a date."

I stare at him. He's gorgeous. Smart. Sweet.

And I'm … well, I'm kind of a bitch.

"Why?"

He looks confused. Surprised almost.

"Why do you want to go out with me?"

"Do you really need me to state the obvious?"

"Aside from the fact that I make your dick hard."

He likes that. I see it from the flare in his eyes.

"You do make my dick hard. Painfully hard."

I roll my eyes. "I'm serious."

"So am I."

"I have been nothing but a bitch to you from day one."

"Maybe I'm a masochist."

"Jack …" I sigh.

He chuckles. "Okay. Yeah, you can be a bitch. But believe it or not, I like that about you, Audrey. I like that you don't take shit from me or anyone. But that's not all you are. You can be funny when you want to be."

"I'm also a loner."

"Me too." He smiles. "Don't sell yourself short, Audrey. You're kind. I see the way you are with my Eleven."

"Just because I like your cat doesn't mean I'm a good person."

"No, but taking her in when you thought she was lost does. And I think you're forgetting the time you broke into my apartment because you were worried that I was hurt." He's smirking.

"You're an ass."

"I do have a nice ass. But yours is better." He squeezes my butt with his hand.

I like this playful side of him. I like it a whole lot.

But I still shouldn't go out with him.

I press my hand to his chest. "I can't date you, Jack."

It's his turn to sigh. "One date, Audrey. Just give me that. One date, and if that doesn't change your mind about me ... *us* ... then I'll leave you alone. What do you say?"

I stare at him. Beautiful, stunning Jack. Who's ignited something inside of me, making me feel almost alive again.

If I go out with him this one time, then I don't have to do it again. There's nothing saying I have to keep dating him.

Maybe I'll go out with him and think he's a total jackass after spending actual, real time with him. It could stop this thing between us from raging on.

Or it could stoke it further.

I mentally sigh, already knowing what I'm going to say before I do it.

"Okay," I say. "One date. And that's it."

He smiles widely. "That's all I need."

FIFTEEN

I agreed to this date, and I have been antsy about it ever since. I've thought about canceling a hundred or so times over the last twenty-four hours.

I know going out with Jack is a bad idea.

It's breaking all my rules.

But ... a part of me also wants to go out with him.

It's been so long since I just did something simple, like go to dinner with someone.

I figure it can't hurt just this once.

And it doesn't mean I have to do it again.

He said one date, and that's all it will be.

We might not even like each other after this date. Maybe the spark that had ignited between us went out yesterday after our hallway interlude.

Oh, who am I kidding?

I haven't stopped thinking about his hands on me, the way he kissed me, since the moment I left his place.

Pretty sure I dreamed about him last night too.

What I need to do is use this date as a way to stamp out our attraction to each other.

I'm not exactly sure how to do that ... but I figure that I'll think of something when the time comes.

I've always been a fast thinker on my feet. Planning has always been my weakness.

I'm a fly-by-the-pants kind of girl.

Jack said he would pick me up for our date at two p.m. Seems early for a date, so I wonder what we're doing.

Not that it really matters.

Well, it shouldn't matter.

And the sooner we go out, the sooner it'll be over with, and I can come back home.

I'm sitting, waiting for Jack to knock on my door.

I was ready for our date in record time. I'm not wearing any makeup. I haven't in a long time. I have to admit, I do miss the fun of putting on makeup. But when you want to blend in like I do, you don't dress your face up, avoiding attracting any form of attention to it. Not even if going on a date.

Especially when I don't want him to like me any more than he already does.

Jack told me to wear warm clothes and walking shoes for our date. Which works for me. I'm not one for dressing up anymore.

So, I'm wearing jeans and an off-the-shoulder dark blue sweater with a white tank underneath it and my furry tan UGG snow boots.

My parker coat, scarf, and gloves are sitting beside me, ready to be put on.

It snowed again overnight, so it's lying nice and thick on the ground.

There's a knock on my door, and aside from the fact that I'm expecting Jack, I know it's him from the way he knocks.

How pathetic is it that I'm familiar with his knock?

Ugh.

I open the door to him, and he looks beautiful. He has on his usual attire. Instead of a T-shirt under his leather jacket though, he's wearing a dark blue knit sweater.

We unknowingly coordinated our clothes.

My heart does a hard bang in my chest.

"We match." I gesture to his sweater.

He glances at my top and smiles. "Do you want me to go change?"

God, he's so lovely. I hate that.

"No." I shake my head.

"So, you ready to go?" he asks.

"Yeah. Just let me grab my coat."

Leaving the door open, I put on my warm things and slip my wallet and phone in one of the pockets. My rape alarm is already in the pocket.

Taking a rape alarm on a date, how romantic.

But I never leave the house without it. And after my experiences, I would be stupid to do so.

I trust Jack as much as I can trust a person. But you never really know anyone.

"Okay, let's go," I tell him.

He catches hold of my gloved hand, stopping me. "You look real pretty today," he tells me. "But then you always do."

My stomach swoops and dives like a flock of birds are in there.

I really need him to stop being so sweet.

"You do too. Look nice, I mean."

His lips quirk into a smile, lighting up his eyes. He squeezes my hand before letting go. "Come on. Let's go have some fun."

I lock up behind us, and we start walking down the hall, heading for the stairwell.

He gestures to the motorbike helmet that he has in his hand. It's matte black with a design of pink flowers on it. Not his usual all-black helmet that he has.

"You okay on the bike?" he asks me.

"Sure." I shrug. "I've never ridden on one before, but it's just the same as a car, right? But without doors and windows. And a seat belt. So, actually, it's nothing like a car."

Jack chuckles. "You'll be fine. You're safe with me, Audrey."

God, I hope so, my heart whispers—and she doesn't mean the bike.

We exit the building, Jack holding the door open for me like a gentleman, and we walk over to his motorbike.

I have zero clue when it comes to bikes. All I know is that his bike is big and black and has *Triumph* written in silver letters on the side of it.

We stop beside his bike, and Jack hands me the helmet. I take it from him. I had the foresight to do my hair into a loose over-the-shoulder plait, making it easier for me to get the helmet on.

Jack opens a helmet bag fixed to the back of his bike and pulls out his usual helmet.

I've got my helmet on fine, but I'm struggling with the chin strap.

"Here, let me help." Jack stands close in front of me. So close that I can feel the warmth of his minty breath on my face. "It's new, so the strap will be a little stiff."

I freeze—and not from the cold. "The strap is new?"

His smiling eyes meet mine. "Yeah, it came with the new helmet."

"You bought a new helmet?"

"Well, yeah. I only had the one, and I couldn't let you ride without one."

He bought a helmet for me.

He. Bought. A. Helmet. For. Me.

It's not a big deal.

Yes, it is. It's a huge deal!

He must see something in my eyes that prompts him to say, "It's not a big deal, Audrey."

"It's not?"

"You can't ride without a helmet, so I got you one. It's that simple." He shrugs.

Maybe it's not a big deal. Maybe I'm just out of practice at this whole peopling thing.

But still ... he bought this just for me. Yes, it's just a helmet. But it's still a kind and thoughtful thing to do.

Ugh!

I'm only ten minutes into this date with him, and I'm a puddle of melted goo on the floor.

So much for shutting down my attraction to him.

Although, in my defense, he isn't exactly making it easy for me to do so.

He's making it so, so much harder.

And I'm starting to realize that maybe there is no way for me to stop liking Jack.

So, I guess I'm left with the only thing I can do ... make Jack dislike me.

SIXTEEN

Jack parks the bike outside a double-story brick building. It has a covered porch out front with steps leading up to the door. It could almost be a house. I look up at the sign on the building—*Animal Adoption and Rescue Center*.

Huh.

We must be going somewhere nearby.

I clamber off the back of his bike, none too gracefully. My legs feel wobbly.

It has nothing to do with the fact that I had my front pressed up against Jack's back and my arms wrapped around his stomach for the last fifteen minutes.

Oh no, it's totally from the bike ride.

And that was sarcasm if you didn't catch it.

I fiddle with the chin strap, trying to undo it, but it's a tricky little fucker.

Still straddling his bike, Jack removes his gloves and takes off his helmet. He puts it in the helmet bag.

Using his hand, he shoves his hair back off his face. His waves fall into place.

I bet when this helmet comes off my hair, it will be stuck to my head, like a sweaty mess.

He looks perfect.

Gorgeous. Sexy. And so very cool.

He's like a character out of the books I read. All broody and hot. Ex-military, now writer. Alpha with a side of nerdiness that makes all the girls swoon.

But I'm not swooning.

Okay, I'm totally swooning.

I'm stopping now.

Any … minute … now …

Jack swings a long leg over the bike and comes to stand in front of me. "Let me." He brushes my hands away from the strap, which I stalled on, taking over.

His nearness sets me off again.

And I'm standing here, just gawking at him.

Because, you know, he's so damn attractive.

In my defense, any girl would find it hard not to stare at Jack.

It would be like asking the stars not to shine at night. Im-frigging-possible.

The clasp clicks open, freeing me from the helmet. Jack gently pulls the helmet off for me.

"Thanks," I say, hastily smoothing back the strands of hair stuck to my forehead and cheeks.

My cheeks are warm from the helmet heat and the internal heat that I have going on.

I sweep my braid back around over my shoulder, checking that it's still in decent shape.

When I look up, I catch Jack watching me.

"What?" I say self-consciously, giving my braid a tug.

His lips curve into one of those easy smiles of his. Stepping closer, he tucks a strand of hair I missed behind my ear.

Everything inside of me stops.

His finger traces around the outer shell of my ear, making me shiver. "Nothing." He shakes his head, eyes holding mine captive. "I just like looking at you."

Right back at ya, babe.

Obviously, I don't say this.

I just swallow down, feeling every single thing in this moment.

The heat in his eyes. The caress of his warm fingers against my cooling skin. The sentiment of his words.

I'm starting to quickly realize that the feelings I have for Jack aren't just entirely sexual.

And that's not good.

I don't want to feel like this every time he is near me or touches me or says something nice to me.

What I want to feel is nothing at all.

Maybe it was a mistake, coming on this date.

I take a step back away from him, moving my eyes down to the ground.

I don't want to see the disappointment in his eyes that I undoubtedly put there.

You want him to stop liking you. This is the way to do it. Being cold. Acting like a bitch.

Only Jack doesn't deserve any of it.

And now, there's this awful silence between us that not even the noises of passing cars and people walking down the busy street fill.

"So …" I start, needing to say something. "Will your bike be okay, parked here?"

"Here is as good as anywhere." He hangs my helmet on one of the handlebars.

"Will that be safe to leave hanging there?" I ask, gesturing to the helmet.

He only just bought it, and I would hate if someone stole it.

Also, I'm a little attached to it.

Attached to a motorbike helmet. Stupid, I know. Because it's not like I plan on riding on the back of his bike again after today.

It's just that he was sweet to buy it for me. And I really need to stop thinking of Jack as sweet.

"Yeah, it'll be fine."

He seems unconcerned, and I guess it's not like I'm back in Chicago, where you can't leave a piece of gum out without someone stealing it.

"So, where are we going then?" I ask him.

"Here." He tips his head in the direction of the building we're standing outside of.

I give him a confused look. "Here? Why? Are you getting another cat or something?"

He chuckles, and I like the sound.

I like making him happy, yet I'm insistent on making him unhappy, so he'll stop liking me.

For God's sake.

I'm baffling the hell out of myself, so God knows what I'm doing to Jack.

I just need to … what?

Honestly, at this point, I have no frigging clue.

"No," he answers me. "We're here to walk a couple of rescue dogs."

"Walk dogs? So, is … this our date?" I check.

Not that it's a bad thing. But I just figured we would be going to the movies or something like that. Basically, like any other date I've ever gone on in the past.

But then Jack's not like anyone I have ever dated in the past.

He steps closer to me again, but there's caution to his approach. "Yeah. Well, it's the first part of it."

"First part?"

"Yep. First, we'll take a walk with a couple of really cool dogs. And then, afterward, I'll feed you."

A dog-walking date.

It's different. Unconventional.

And I absolutely love it.

I am so totally and undeniably screwed.

Jack holds his hand out to me.

I hesitate here for a second. Staring down at his hand. Strong and gentle, waiting for me.

I feel like this is a now-or-never moment.

Why now, I don't know.

But I feel that if I take his hand and go forward with this date, then there is no turning back for me.

I pull in a breath on a long blink. Then, I tug my glove off and put my hand in Jack's.

Smiling, he curls his fingers around mine. I lift my eyes to his.

He gives my hand a light squeeze. "Let's go in."

I let Jack lead me inside.

We walk into the reception area. The woman standing behind the desk—who I would guess is in her fifties with her graying light-brown hair tied back in a ponytail and surprisingly tanned skin for where we live—smiles widely when she sees Jack.

I know, lady. He has that effect on all of us.

"Hey, Jack," she says.

"Afternoon, Shelly," he greets her. "How are you today?"

"I'm good. So, you've brought us another victim," she says chirpily.

I flinch internally at her word choice—*victim*.

It's stupid that I can still be affected by a single word related to my past, but I am.

Thankfully, I'm a lot better at hiding my emotions than I once was.

"Another victim?" I question quietly at his side.

He glances down at me, a smile touching his lips. "You're my first, I swear."

His attention turns back to Shelly. "Yep. I got you another walker. This is Audrey," he tells her. "Audrey, meet Shelly."

"Hi," I say.

"You walked rescue dogs before?" she asks me.

"Nope. Total newbie."

"No worries at all," she says kindly. "It's just the same as walking any regular dogs—with just a few rules."

"Don't worry; I'll bring her up to speed," Jack tells Shelly.

She nods. "Well, I just need you to fill out this form, so I can add you to our system." She slides a form across the counter along with a pen. "I'll go ready the dogs for you while you fill this out."

Picking up the pen, I stare down at the form. It's nothing major, just basic information—name, address, phone number, questions, like if I've ever been charged with animal cruelty. The sort of things you would expect from an animal rescue center.

But that last question sticks out to me.

No, I've never been cruel to an animal. I never would be. I love animals.

But animals were killed because some psycho thought it was a way to declare his twisted-up sense of love for me.

I always fear that another animal could die again because of me.

Another person.

I guess finding that rat in my apartment the other day had bothered me even more than I realized.

Sighing, I start filling out the form.

I put the pen down when I'm finished completing it and look up and to my right to find Jack leaning against the wall, watching me.

"You're staring again."

He shrugs, unbothered.

I like that about him. How he's unafraid to show what he's feeling or thinking. Literally nothing seems to faze him.

"Did I get this wrong?" he asks softly.

His question surprises me.

"Get what wrong?" I turn my body toward his.

"The date. Bringing you here. Should I have taken you elsewhere?"

"No." I frown. "What makes you say that?"

"Because you look unhappy."

"I always look unhappy. I have resting bitch face," I try to joke.

He pushes off the wall and takes a step closer, leaning his forearms on the counter. "Did I get this wrong, Audrey?" he asks me again.

Only … I feel like he's also asking me something else, but I'm not sure exactly what that is.

So, I answer the one question I know for sure he asked me.

I shake my head. "No, Jack. If anything, you got it *too* right."

"Here we are." Shelly's voice comes from behind me along with the sound of claws skittering across the hardwood floor.

I turn and see the two cutest dogs ever.

One is a Weimaraner, and the other is a gray-and-white Siberian husky with the brightest blue eyes that I have ever seen on an animal before. They actually remind me of Jack's eyes.

Both dogs are wearing luminous vests that say *Adopt Me* on them.

How anyone could ever abandon these beautiful dogs, I will never know.

They're both eager to come over to us, but Shelly has a good handle on them, considering they're strong dogs.

I get down to my knees as they approach, giving them both strokes and fusses, getting face licks in return, making me laugh.

I like animals so much better than people.

Well, maybe except for the guy standing beside me. But I'm not even allowing my thoughts to go there. Not right now anyway. I can figure out my tangled-up feelings for Jack later—when I'm alone and away from his charming self.

"Sorry to drop and run," Shelly says, handing the leads over to Jack. "Ronnie has just brought a dog in. Needs my help."

"Go," he tells her. "We'll be back in an hour or so."

She nods and disappears back to where she came from.

"Ronnie?" I ask.

"Her husband. They run this place together."

"So, which doggy is mine to walk?" I ask him.

"You choose. But I'll tell you, Pork Chop is a puller."

"Pork Chop." I laugh. "That might be the best name I've ever heard. And Pork Chop is which dog?"

"The Weimaraner."

"I'll take the husky then." I grin.

Chuckling, Jack hands me the husky's lead.

"So, what is my doggy called?" I ask as we begin walking to the door.

"Gary," Jack says.

"Gary!" I burst out laughing. "I expected him to have a super-cool name, like Storm or Loki. Not Gary."

Jack laughs as well. "Gary is cool … kind of."

"Said no one ever," I joke. "Aw, Gary, bud." I pat his head. "Thank God you're gorgeous because you got shafted in the name department."

Not that Gary gives a fudge what I'm saying. His sole focus is on the door and getting outside. Can't blame the little dude. I'm sure the people here are good to the dogs, but they probably also spend a lot of time in their cages, waiting for someone to take them to their forever home.

It makes my heart hurt for them.

Jack opens the door. He tries to let me through first with Gary, but Pork Chop is not having any of it and yanks Jack through the door.

Laughing, I catch hold of the door with my hand, letting Gary through first.

I have a feeling this walk is going to be a lot of fun.

We set off in the direction of a walking trail close to the center.

"So, you do this often?" I ask Jack.

"As much as I can."

"You're a good guy, Jack Canti." I smile at him.

For the first time since I've known Jack, I actually see a look of shyness on his face, his cheeks reddening a touch.

If I wasn't already half-gone for him, I would be now.

Jack tries to shrug it off, like the cool guy he is, but I know better. "I like to walk, and these guys need walking."

"How come you don't have a dog?" I ask him.

"One, I don't think Eleven would be happy if I brought one home. And two, dogs demand more time than I can give to one right now. But it is nice to do this, to help the dogs out in this way."

"I get that," I tell him. Doing something for others leaves you with a sense of worth. "So, tell me the rules for walking these guys."

"Okay, so no letting them off their leads unless in a designated area where you can do so. No letting them chase wildlife. And always scoop the poop."

My face scrunches up at that thought. "Okay. Do you have poop bags?"

He taps his jacket pocket with his hand, grinning. "Yep. Oh, and one thing I forgot to mention ... Pork Chop might be the puller, but Gary is the shitter."

"What do you mean, he's the shitter?" My eyes narrow, and Jack's grin widens.

"Gary likes to save all his shits up for his walks. Minimum he'll take on a walk is two."

"Two craps is the minimum!" I stare down at the dog. "What is wrong with you?" Then, I look back to Jack. "What is wrong with him?"

Jack is howling with laughter by this point.

"It's not funny!" I gesticulate. "Right, that's it! We're swapping dogs." I hold Gary's lead out to Jack. "I'll take Pork Chop the puller, and you can have Gary the pooper!"

"No can do." Jack wipes his laughing eyes. "You'll hurt Gary's feelings if you switch now."

"What?" I look down at Gary again. He's staring up at me with those gorgeous Jack eyes, and now, I just feel mean. "Fine," I huff. I keep up the pretense of being annoyed, but seriously, how can I be with this cutie staring at me? And I am talking about Gary, not Jack.

Or maybe I do mean them both.

"Bring me on a date and have me picking up dog crap."

Jack chuckles. "Baby, it is nothing but the high life with me."

"Hmm," I grumble, steadfastly ignoring the way he just called me baby and the way my body reacted to it. "You'd better feed me good after this. Well, that is, if Gary and his hundreds of shits don't kill my appetite."

"It's not hundreds. Probably around five."

"Five!" I shriek.

Jack sputters out a laugh. "Kidding. Four at the most."

I frown at him.

His grin is unrepentant, and it lights up his whole face and those stunning eyes of his.

I have to fight a smile from creeping onto my own face.

"You're an ass."

"A hot ass though."

I shake my head, still fighting that damn smile.

"Okay, how about I scoop the poop for you? It's the least I can do since you agreed to come on a date with me."

"Wow. And there I was, thinking chivalry was a thing of the past."

"What can I say? I'm the last remaining gentleman." His shoulder presses against mine as he leans closer, bringing his mouth to my ear. "But not in bed, Audrey. I am most definitely not a fucking gentleman in bed."

Holy. Sexual. Shivers.

How the hell am I supposed to resist him when he says stuff like that to me?

In one breath, sweet and kind. And then in the other, hot and alpha and so very fucking sexy.

He's like the perfect combination of everything I would ever want in a man.

It's in moments like this that I am absolutely, positively sure that someone upstairs hates me.

Gary tugs on the lead, wanting us to follow Jack and Pork Chop. So, I walk on, letting him lead the way, while I try to sort out my jumbled-up mess of thoughts.

SEVENTEEN

I, Audrey Hayes, am in love.

With a dog called Gary.

He's so sweet and adorable.

After our walk was over, leaving him at the adoption center was hard to do. Honestly, I would have taken him home with me if I could. If I didn't have to worry about him being alone all day while I was at work—and also his safety while living with me. Bad things seem to happen to animals around me.

Truthfully, I worry for Eleven at times. Worry that my bad juju will get her, but it's hard to turn her away when she shows up, and selfishly, I love having the company when she's around.

It makes me feel less lonely.

And Gary must have been having a good time with me, or maybe he heard my words of complaint because he only took one poop while we were out walking. I am going to go with the theory that it's because he likes me.

I've already signed up to come walk Gary on my lunch break from work tomorrow. The center is only five minutes away from the library, which is perfect.

It makes me feel guilty that I didn't know about this before. I could have been walking Gary and other dogs like him the whole time I have been living in Jackson.

But I know now, and that's what I am going to do, going forward. It's a perfect arrangement for a loner like me. I get company and exercise with Gary, which is something we both need, and I'm not risking getting close to or hurting anyone in the process. It's a win-win.

Now, if only I could figure out this thing with Jack—how to handle my feelings for him, how to shut them down, and how to turn off his attraction to me—then things would be A-OK.

Jack reserved us a table at the local Japanese restaurant. I absolutely love Japanese food. It's another tick in his good box. *Sigh.*

The restaurant is close by the adoption center, so we leave his bike where it's parked and walk the short distance.

I haven't been in here before. Well, I haven't been anywhere in Jackson, except for the library, coffee shop, and supermarket.

We approach the restaurant. Jack opens the door, letting me in first.

It's toasty warm in here, and the smells are amazing. My stomach rumbles eagerly. It has been so long since I ate in a restaurant.

I take my gloves off, pocketing them. After unwinding my scarf from around my neck, I unzip my coat and remove it.

There's a coat rack by the door, so I hang my things on it. Jack does the same.

Looking around, I feel a little underdressed to be here in my jeans, sweater, and boots. The other diners are dressed much nicer.

But there is nothing I can do about it now, and it's not like I'm here to impress anyone.

Yeah, sure you're not, Audrey.

Anyway, Jack's seen me way more dressed down than this. The guy has seen me dressed in sweatpants, for God's sake.

Even still, I can't help but straighten my sweater out, and then I tidy my hair as best I can, tucking away stray hairs behind my ears.

"Stop worrying. You look beautiful." Jack's hand slips into mine, giving it a gentle squeeze.

My eyes lift to his. "I'm not worried." *Liar.*

His brow lifts, his expression one of skepticism.

"Fine." I sigh. "I just feel a tad underdressed for this place."

"I never took you to be a person who cared what others thought."

"I'm not." The old me … she would have cared though. "But I also don't like to stand out either."

Jack regards me with those clever eyes of his. Like he is reading my thoughts.

Thankfully, the hostess approaches, breaking the moment.

She's around my age and very pretty.

"Hi, guys." She smiles at Jack, not me. I can't even be mad because I get it. I would be the same if I were her. "Do you have a reservation?" she asks him.

"Yes," he tells her. "Canti. Table for two."

She glances down at the listings on the hostess stand, running her finger down the paper. "Yep, here you are." She grabs two menus and says, "Follow me, please."

She leads us over to a table for two by the window. Jack pulls the chair out for me.

"Still being a gentleman?" I tease, taking the seat, referring back to his earlier comment that practically set my libido on fire. A fire that still hasn't gone out.

Still, I shouldn't have brought it up because saying stuff like that is only going to move things with him in a direction that it shouldn't go.

Like Jack and me having sex.

Jack sits in the seat across from me, taking his menu from the hostess, his eyes fixed solely on me. "You ready for me to stop being a gentleman? Because we can leave right now and go back to your apartment."

To bed.

His meaning is crystal clear, and the sexual tension thickens the air between us.

I can't help the smile that tips up my lips and the words that leave my mouth. "You have to feed me first."

So, apparently, I am going to have sex with him tonight.

Seems my sense and life rules got lost somewhere along that trail we walked the dogs on before.

That, or the sight of Jack's tight ass walking in front of me in those jeans woke the old Audrey up. She never had any qualms with talking about sex openly. Was confident with men. Until …

Nope, not going there right now.

I am enjoying this little game the two of us are suddenly playing though. It makes me feel … alive.

The old me is back for the night, and I honestly like it.

There is nothing clean about the grin that Jack gives me. He rests his elbows on the table, linking his fingers together, stare still fixed on me.

I can't look away from him either. I feel like it's only the two of us in the world now.

It's exhilarating and utterly fucking terrifying.

A shadow falls over the table, breaking the moment between us. Leaving whatever Jack was about to say a mystery.

"What can I get you both to drink?" asks the waiter.

Jack and I both order beers, and the waiter leaves to get our drinks.

I stare out the window, needing to collect my thoughts for a minute. Wanting to gain at least a smidgen of composure back. I've never felt so unbalanced yet more like my old self than I do around Jack.

It's started snowing again. I watch the flakes drift lazily to the ground.

"Will your bike be okay?" I gesture to the weather.

"The bike will be fine. You and I will most likely have damp asses from the ride back home though."

I'm already damp, just from looking at you, so no worries there.

I chuckle. More at my own dirty thought than what Jack said.

"I should get a car really," he says. "Having the bike in this climate isn't exactly ideal."

I can't imagine Jack driving anything other than his motorbike. Although a car would be nice to ride in on the way home. A wet ass is not high on my list of things to have.

"Have you always ridden motorbikes?" I ask him.

"Pretty much. Although I didn't get to ride so much when I was in the military."

"Too busy driving tanks?" I smile, resting my chin in my hand.

"Something like that."

"Maybe you don't have to get rid of the bike. You could keep it to use in the summer and just have a car for winter."

"Does this place even have a summer?" he asks, leaning back in his chair.

"So I've been told." I shrug. "I have yet to see it."

"How long have you lived here?"

I feel my spine stiffen at the question.

Relax, Audrey. It's a perfectly normal question.

"Six months," I tell him. Even I can hear the caution in my voice though. So, I try to cover it up with my own question. "What made a motorbiking guy like you move to snowy Jackson?"

"Research."

"For your book?"

"Mmhmm."

"You write fictional crime books, right? So, what are you working on right now?"

If he has switched to nonfiction and is writing a real-life crime book, I'm out of here.

"You looked me up?" He grins.

"Your books. Not you. Don't get a big head. I work in a library. It would be weird if I didn't look your books up."

He's still smirking, and I feel like I'm digging myself into a hole.

"And?"

"What?"

"What did you think?"

"I didn't read them. Crime is not my thing."

He nods, as if remembering me telling him this when he first told me what books he writes.

"But they looked good. You first published when you were still in the military, right?"

"Yeah."

"Did you always want to be a writer?"

The waiter brings our beers over, interrupting, and asks to take our orders. We've barely looked at the menu. But after a quick scan, Jack orders the yakitori, and I decide on the seared scallops.

"To answer your question," Jack says after taking a sip of his beer, "yeah, I always wanted to be a writer. My father … didn't see it as a viable career path. He was ex-military. He pushed me in that direction, and I allowed him to."

"But you keep writing."

"Yeah. My—" He suddenly stops, cutting his words off.

"Your what?" I ask out of curiosity.

He shakes his head, as if clearing his thoughts. "Sorry, I lost my train of thought there for a minute. I was just going to say … my friend, he was the one who got me published. I kept writing while I was away. I would send him the chapters I had written. He kept them all. Typed them up and submitted them to a publisher without me knowing." He laughs to himself. "I got my first book deal because of him."

Listening to him, I get the impression that he's hiding something. Maybe that the *he* was actually a *she*, an ex-girlfriend, and he doesn't want to discuss past women while trying to get in this current woman's panties.

"Wow. That's one good friend. Sneaky"—I chuckle—"but good."

"Yeah. He is good. The best."

"Where is he now?" I take a sip of my beer.

"Gone."

"Gone? Where?"

He blinks, looking past me. "Australia."

I feel like there is a story there. About him and some girl who left him to go to Australia. But I'm not going to dig for more information. I've done enough asking about his past for the night. If I'm not careful, he's going to start asking me questions about my life.

"Wow. Well, thank God for airplanes, right?"

He just smiles in response.

A silence descends on us. Surprisingly, it's not one I created. Something is on his mind right now, but I'm not going to ask what it is.

The jealous girl in me doesn't want to know if he is thinking about a long-lost love.

Ugh.

See, this is why I stay away from people. They're too much hassle.

"Um … so thanks for bringing me here," I say for the sake of saying something. "It's a nice place."

His broody eyes come back to mine. "You don't have to thank me."

I shrug. "I'm really enjoying myself, walking the dogs as well. Gary and Pork Chop are adorable. Do you know their stories?" I ask him. "How did they end up at the shelter?"

"Pork Chop's owner passed away, and Gary was a stray. Found wandering around the streets. Shelly said he was in bad shape when they brought him in."

My poor Gary.

I have a heartbreaking vision of a skinny, shabby-looking Gary, confused, lost, and wondering why his owners left him alone. Why they didn't want him anymore.

"Hey. He's okay now." Jack reaches over, covering my hand with his.

I start at the contact.

"Shelly and Ron are good people. They will find him a forever home soon enough," he adds in a soothing voice.

"I know." I blink clear whatever emotion he saw in my eyes that prompted him to reassure me like that.

I'm really wishing my hair were down now, so I could hide my face with the thick curtain of it.

Clearing my throat, I slide my hand out from under his in the pretense of picking up my beer bottle.

I put it to my lips, taking a long drink. I can't believe how upset I got then at the thought of Gary being alone.

Maybe because you're alone, and you know how it feels.

Yeah, but my being alone is my choice.

But is it really? Or is it a necessity that arose from a situation you hadn't caused?

Oh, fuck off, subconscious.

I put my beer down. Keeping ahold of it, I pick at the edge of the label with my thumbnail.

"Hey, just a thought …" I start, needing to take the conversation into humor. "Maybe this is why Eleven keeps escaping from your apartment … because you keep coming home, smelling of dogs. She probably thinks you're cheating on her with those damn dogs, so she packs up her shit and leaves you." I smirk.

He barks out a laugh. "Funny too." He taps a finger to the table. "Along with a good heart." He catches my eyes. "You can add those to your list of good qualities."

A hollowness seeps into my chest.

Because he's wrong. So very wrong. I am none of those things. Well, maybe I am funny. But I definitely don't have a good heart. Maybe I used to have one once upon a time ago.

But now … no.

To have a good heart, you would need to use it, and I put that muscle to rest a long time ago.

I look away, down to the label I'm picking at.

"I've embarrassed you." His deep voice touches my skin.

"You haven't."

"If you want your lie to be convincing, maybe wear makeup next time. It'd cover your red cheeks."

My face is warm but not from embarrassment. More from … disappointment. Disheartenment that he sees something in me that's not there anymore. Or maybe he just sees what he wants. Most people do.

Folks can create an illusion of the person they want you to be, and when you fail to live up to it, the truth is somehow *your* fault.

Or it's the reverse, and *we* create the illusion. Make people think we're something we're not in order for them to try to catch and keep us.

The very trait of a serial killer. Only they don't try to keep. They take. And take. And take some more.

And me … well, I am none of those things. A creation of circumstances. An anomaly.

What you see is what you get. A bitch most days. And a hollow carcass for the rest.

"How come you don't wear makeup?" His question jolts me back to the now.

My brow furrows. I don't know why, but his words irk me. I sit taller in my seat. "Should I? Is wearing makeup a requirement for women?"

Why am I being so bitchy all of a sudden?

Because you are a bitch, remember?

He gives me a confused look. "No …" he says slowly, probably wondering where my snit has come from. "It isn't a requirement, merely an observation. Most women wear it, right? You don't. I simply wondered why." He gives a small lift of his gentle shoulders.

"Do you like your women to wear makeup?" Part of me already knows the answer to this question. Because if he did, he wouldn't be sitting here with me right now. So, why I'm asking, I have no clue.

"My women?" He laughs. It's loud and bright. It loosens up the tightness in my chest. "Do you mean, like a harem? Don't have one of them, sadly."

I roll my eyes, batting away his humor. "I meant, women you're attracted to."

"Ah. Well, I'm attracted to you."

"And I don't wear makeup."

"Guess you have your answer then."

Fuck. Walked into that one, didn't I?

I hate that my insides warm up like a mug of cocoa.

Ignoring his words, I rest my chin in my hand and look directly at him. "So, to make you dislike me, I need to start wearing makeup?" I grin.

Another laugh. "Honestly, nothing could make me dislike you at this point, pretty girl."

Pretty girl?

He called me pretty girl.

Cue my melting heart.

Stop. Don't get distracted by silly pet names, Audrey.

Focus.

"You sure about that?" I push.

"Well, I'm never wholly sure about anything. But, yeah, I'm almost sure that nothing could stop me from liking you."

I tilt my head to the side, thinking. "What about smelly feet?"

"What about them?"

"Well, what if I have stinky-ass feet?"

"Do you?"

"No."

"Then, it's a moot point."

Argh! Stop being so damn cute, man.

"But what if they did smell? Like rotten, decades-old cheese."

He leans back in his chair, hand still curled around his beer bottle. His lips lifted at one side.

He looks so hot right now.

Ack. Who am I kidding? He always looks hot.

That is the reason I'm sitting here with him. Because of his damn hotness.

And his kindness. And sweet personality.

Jack drums the fingers of his free hand on the tabletop. "If you want to try and make this work,

Audrey, then give me something that's actually true, not a hypothetical."

I sit up straighter. My brows pulling together in confusion. "For what to work?"

"Your attempt to turn me off you. That is what you're going for here, right? What you said a moment ago." He leans forward, elbows on the table. Holding the bottle by its neck, he brings it close to his lips. "So, hit me with your worst. What is *the* worst thing about Audrey Hayes? Something so closet-hiding hideous that even I, the guy who thinks you're the single hottest woman I have ever seen in my life, would be turned off by it. And make it a good one. Please."

His eyes appraise me. Almost goading me.

"People have died because of me."

Jack's eyes seem to freeze. Like when you pause the channel on TV. He's just staring at me for what feels like the longest moment, which is probably, in reality, mere seconds.

But then I did just drop *that* bomb on the table.

Holy fuck.

I actually said that.

I can't believe I said that.

I'm reeling.

Where the hell did that come from?

My heart is going nuts in my chest.

I'm going to hyperventilate.

Well, I did want to put an end to this thing between us. And that was a surefire way to do it.

It's like calling out the wrong name during sex.

Nope, it's worse.

Telling a guy on the first date that you attract death? A definite no-no.

He's going to think that I'm crazy.

Good.

Really, Audrey? Is that honestly what you want? For this thing with him to stop?

Maybe not.

But what I want and what is necessary is not the same thing.

Jack finally blinks and puts the bottle to his lips. He takes a drink and then places it back down to the table, cradling it in his big hands.

"And here I was, thinking you were going to say something like … you'd cheated on an exam."

I laugh out loud. It's a maniacal-sounding laugh.

Cheated on an exam. Ha. If only.

"Nope. Never cheated on an exam. You?"

"Once. Tenth grade. I was failing math. Some kid in our school hacked into the school computers and got the answers. I paid him twenty bucks for a copy."

We go from talking about me being a harbinger of death directly to talking about his tenth-grade math test.

If this isn't weird, then I don't know what is.

"Did you get caught?" I ask.

"Nope. And I'm also not proud of that fact either," he emphasizes.

"So, is cheating on your school test your worst?" I ask him.

Jack shakes his head, eyes fixed on mine. "No."

You can tell a lot from one word. And that singular no he just said spoke volumes.

"Want to tell me about it?"

His gaze lifts to mine. "Want to expand on you being the reason people have died?"

I shake my head.

"That's what I thought."

There's a beat of silence before I ask, "So, did it work?" My voice is scratchy. Sounds like it hasn't been used in years.

"Putting me off you?" Jack checks.

"Yes." I take a swig of my beer, trying to appear unaffected by whatever he might say.

But the truth is that I am going to be affected by his answer either way.

Yes or no.

I want him. I shouldn't want him.

The dark, broken parts of me want Jack's light so very badly.

But the smart part of my brain says no.

If you like him, then stay away from him.

I can't win this war that is waging in my head when it comes to Jack.

I guess there is nothing left for me to do but accept whatever is going to happen.

Jack laughs a soft, sad kind of sound. "We're not so different, you and me, Audrey."

"In what way?"

"People have died because of me too."

EIGHTEEN

The rest of dinner went as it should. Normal conversation. Likes, dislikes.

No more talk of death.

I was careful to make sure it didn't stray into the path of my past. Even though I was desperate to know about Jack's. Well, more so of what he'd said.

"People have died because of me too."

But our waiter appeared with our meals, interrupting before anything more could be said. And once our food was served and we were alone again, I opened my mouth to ask just exactly what he'd meant with that statement, but something stopped me.

Because hadn't I said pretty much the same thing to him and then flat-out refused to expand on it?

He doesn't have to tell me a damn thing. And if I had asked him to explain his words, I would have only been putting myself in danger of having to do the same.

So, I said nothing and let the conversation over dinner take a normal turn.

Now, we're heading back home on his motorcycle. My ass only a little chilly from the snow. Jack did a good

SAMANTHA TOWLE

job of cleaning off the seat before we got on it. Although my helmet was as cold as hell. Jack offered me his to wear, but it was too big for my head.

So, he pulled out a beanie from his helmet bag, put it on my head, and put my helmet on top.

I know my hair is going to look a mess when I take the beanie off. But I'm warm, and the beanie smells like Jack, so it's hard to be bothered by the thought of fluffy hair.

The date is almost over. It's not like it matters how my hair looks now.

No, that's not a pang of disappointment in my chest at the thought of my time with Jack coming to an end.

Okay, it totally is.

But who says the date has to be over the moment we get back?

I could invite him in for a drink.

And sex.

I mean, it was pretty clear from the conversation— not the one about death—that sex was on the menu for tonight.

And despite his death line, I want to.

I can't exactly be turned off by what he said ... as I said the exact same thing.

Maybe Jack hasn't attracted the attention of a serial murderer, like me, but he was in the military.

People die at the hands of soldiers. And soldiers die at the hand of war. Many, many lives are lost because of war.

And Jack was stationed in Syria, where a war was happening.

It would be a surprise to me if that wasn't what he meant when he made that statement.

And my gut tells me that Jack is nothing like Tobias.

Nothing in the way he behaves gives any indication that he's a total psycho.

Not that I ever knew Tobias. I said hello to him a couple of times, and that was it.

How scary is it that a man I didn't even know terrorized and changed my life forever?

Nope. I refuse to let my mind veer down that path tonight.

I've had a nice time with Jack.

I'm not letting my past take that from me as well.

Jack steers his bike into his usual parking spot outside of our building and turns off the engine.

Holding on to Jack's arms, I clamber off the bike and manage to undo and get the helmet off for the first time on my own, pulling the beanie off with it.

I retrieve it from the inside of the helmet and offer it back to Jack.

Climbing off the bike with his usual grace, he takes it from me and puts it in the helmet bag along with his own helmet.

"What should I do with this one?" I ask him.

"Keep it," he tells me.

"Keep it?"

"Yeah. It's yours. I bought it for you."

"But …"

His hand cups my cheek, his thumb resting over my lips. "It's yours." He smiles. "It's my way of making sure you ride with me again one day."

I'll ride you if you want.

Jesus, Audrey.

Since when did I turn into a sex-starved nympho?

Since Jack, apparently.

"Okay." It's my turn to smile. "Well, thank you."

"No thanks needed." He stares at me. His eyes darken. It … looks like he wants to kiss me.

I want him to kiss me.

I already know what it feels like to have Jack's lips on mine, his tongue in my mouth, and I want to feel it again.

So very frigging badly.

I would normally lick my lips, giving him the indication that I want what I think he wants, too, if it didn't mean I would lick his thumb still resting against my lips. And licking his thumb would just be way too weird, even for me.

So, I try to convey with my eyes that I want him to remove his thumb and replace it with his lips.

Snowflakes start to fall again.

Jack blinks and then glances up at the sky. "Come on. Let's get you inside."

He removes his hand from my face, and my skin instantly goes cold.

I try not to sigh at the loss of both his hand and the kiss that never happened.

Why didn't he kiss me just then?

Did I get that moment wrong?

Maybe he didn't want to kiss me at all, and it was all in my head.

Or maybe I did actually manage to put him off me throughout the course of this date.

Well, talking about death over dinner would do it.

The pang of disappointment that hits my gut is hard, and it tells me everything I need to know about how I feel about this fact.

Well, I have no one to blame but myself, and it's probably for the best.

And I'll be sure to convey that message to my libido when I'm lying in bed later tonight. Horny and alone.

For a girl who doesn't want to feel anything anymore, especially not for a man, I'm doing a shit-as-hell job of keeping my hormones and emotions in check.

Jack holds open the door to our building, allowing me through first. We walk up the stairs in silence.

The quiet between us is beginning to put me on edge. Not knowing what he's thinking. Not knowing what he's going to say.

Is he just going to walk me to my door, thank me for a nice evening, and then walk away?

Ugh. Getting given the good-night handshake is going to be the worst.

But in the end, it'd be the right thing.

This thing with Jack would be a disaster.

I'm a disaster. Hence the reason that I've spent the last six months distancing myself from everyone around me. Having a person in my life would not be a good idea. Especially not a man like Jack.

I'm pretty much resigned by the time we reach my apartment door.

I tug off my gloves, get my keys from my pocket, and unlock the door.

Facing him, my fingers curled around the handle, I say, "So ... thanks for today. I had fun."

"Me too," he says, holding my stare.

I press down on the handle, opening the door. "Well, good night then."

"Audrey." The low baritone in his voice sends a shiver hurtling through my body.

I turn back to him.

"That's not how this date ends."

My heart starts to pitter-patter in my chest. "No?"

"No."

He steps into my space, and I suck in a breath.

"So … how does it end?"

Jack takes my head in his hands, tilting my face up to his. "It doesn't. It starts with a kiss."

He covers my lips with his.

It's like a bomb detonates around us, the force shoving us together.

There is something electric between Jack and me. Something confusing and scary and exhilarating.

Something I don't know how to control. How to stop. Or if I even want to.

I have never wanted anyone the way I want him.

My fingers thread into his hair. He groans against my mouth.

I press my body to his in response.

His tongue slides between my lips, into my mouth, and all of my synapses fry.

Distantly, I hear the click of a door opening. Then, I'm moving backward.

Jack picks me up. I wrap my legs around his waist.

The door shuts, and my back is pressed up against it.

The kiss is raw, electric. It has the sweetness of anticipation and the sharpness of desperation.

We're tongues and teeth. Nipping, biting, sucking.

We're on a whole other level from our first kiss yesterday.

Because I know, this time, Jack and I are going to have sex.

His hands flex restlessly against my ass. Fingers gripping, grasping.

I'm panting into his mouth, needing more of him. Wanting to feel him.

There are too many clothes between us.

I reach for the zipper on his jacket, yanking it down. I shove his jacket off his shoulders.

Jack stops kissing me, putting me to my feet. I push his jacket the rest of the way off, hearing it drop to the floor.

It's only then that I register my apartment is dark. Only the moonlight coming from my living room windows gives a muted glow.

It is surprising to me that I haven't turned the light on yet. Being in the dark is not something I can usually cope with.

But still, I don't reach for the switch.

Maybe having Jack here is comforting to me. Maybe he makes me feel safe.

Or maybe I'm just so damn horny that all my other senses, fears, and worries have taken a backseat.

Jack unwinds the scarf from around my neck. Then, he unzips my coat, taking his time. The sound is erotically loud in the silence of my apartment.

Then, my coat is gone from my body.

Jack stares down at me in the dark. Not touching me.

My body is thrumming with anticipation. My breaths uneven.

He lifts a hand. Fingertips gently skim the bare skin on my shoulder, revealed from my off-the-shoulder sweater.

One of his fingers hooks on the straps of my tank and bra, curling around, tugging me even closer.

My breasts crush up against his hard chest.

Then, our mouths go at it again. Fusing together.

The kiss goes from zero to sixty in less than a second.

My hands fumble for his jeans.

Jack grabs my hands, stopping me, pinning them and me back up against the door.

He kisses my neck, his tongue sliding down along my collarbone, leaving a hot trail of desire in its wake.

He releases my hands and takes hold of my braid. Winding it around his hand, he tugs me to his mouth, kissing me briefly but firmly.

Then, he pulls the tie from the end of my hair. His fingers make quick work of freeing it.

My eyes drift shut at the feel of his hands as they move over my head, my hair loose and flowing over my shoulders.

He fingers a lock of it. "This is the first time I've seen your hair down." His voice is thick, laced with desire and some other unnamed emotion. "So fucking beautiful," he rasps softly.

I can tell that he means what he says.

I know that even if nothing sexual happened with Jack and me tonight—well, aside from the fact that I might cry with frustration—I would know that he meant what he said in this moment.

And it causes an ache in my chest.

Because he hasn't seen me.

Not all of me.

He doesn't know the real me.

And if he did, he wouldn't think that I was beautiful anymore.

I have scars.

Ugly scars that I can never get rid of.

On my skin.

And inside of my soul.

I'm damaged.

Physically and mentally.

I am not beautiful. But right now, I so desperately want to be. For him more than myself.

But I've seen the worst side of life, and I can never come back from that.

There is no happy ending for me.

But maybe I can have just this one moment with Jack.

This single moment of peace.

Where my mind is full of only him and the way he makes me feel.

Jack pulls my sweater over my head, leaving me in my tank.

He kisses me again, wrapping his arms around my waist, bringing my body back to his.

My hips are restless, shifting. I need to feel him against me. Inside me.

His hand moves lower to my ass. Grabbing hold, he yanks me against his erection, giving me the contact I so urgently need.

I hear a hot gasp and realize it came from me.

Jack sucks on my tongue, and I am putty in his hands.

He circles his hips against mine, and I moan into his mouth. My fingers slide into his hair, gripping the strands.

I'm stuck between a solid door and a rock-hard body, and there is nowhere else I want to be right now than here.

My hands roam, needing skin. I grapple with his sweater, tugging it up.

Jack gets the message, letting me go so he can pull it over his head in that sexy way that he does.

I admire him in the muted light. The hard lines of his chest. His hard-earned abs. The strip of dark hair that follows the sculpted V down into his jeans.

I reach for his jeans, wanting them off. I tug open the button. Dragging the zipper down, I slide my hand inside, desperate to touch him.

The part of him that I need inside me more than I need my next breath.

My fingers slide into the waistband of his underwear, seeking.

When my fingertips make contact with the head of his cock, Jack hisses a breath in between his teeth.

My fingers graze down the soft skin of his rock-hard shaft before curling around his cock and giving it a squeeze.

"Fuck," Jack curses.

His hand grabs the back of my head, bringing me back to his mouth, and he kisses the hell out of me.

I start jacking him off, loving the low groans he makes into my mouth.

The kiss moves from hot to frantic in seconds.

His hands find my breasts, cupping them over my tank and bra beneath it.

My nipples pebble against the drag of the fabric of my bra as he runs his thumb over one of them.

The back of my head hits the wall. A sigh of pleasure escaping me.

"You like that?" His low voice makes me hot in all the right places.

"Yes," I whisper.

The next thing I know, his hands take hold of the hem of my tank top, trying to lift it up, and that is when everything goes to hell in a handbasket.

NINETEEN

"**N**o!" I yell, shoving his hands away from me.

Jack practically jumps back from me, a look of surprise on his handsome face.

And I can't blame him. We went from sizzling hot to freezing cold in less than a second.

"I'm sorry," he starts, his hands going up in the air. "I—"

"It's not your fault," I cut him off. Shame is coating me like thick black oil. "You didn't do anything wrong. It's me … I can't …" *How the hell do I say this? How do I tell him that I can't get naked with him from the waist up and not explain the reason?*

"You can't what, Audrey?" His voice is soft, calm, measured. Like the way you would speak to a frightened animal.

It makes me feel as pathetic as I know I am.

I don't know what to say. I stare down at the floor, trying to find the right words.

But there are none.

Jack takes a step closer, but he doesn't reach for me.

And I won't lie. It hurts.

I hate that *I* put this distance between us.

That my past put this distance between us.

"Nothing has to happen tonight. Not until you're ready."

I look back up at him. "I am ready. I want you, but …"

"Talk to me …" he urges softly.

"I can't …" I press a hand against the area just beneath my breasts, at the top of my stomach, where the ugliest physical part of me resides.

I close my eyes and pull in a strengthening breath.

Why didn't I think of this before? That getting naked with him would be par for the course before having sex with him?

Because I'm stupid.

I was so blinded by lust because I wanted him so very badly that I didn't think this out at all.

Moron.

"I can't get naked with you. Well, the top half of me can't." I curl my fingers into my tank top, hating the feel of the lumpy skin beneath it. "My bottom half is fine." *God, I sound like a total fucktard.* "And I can't tell you why, so don't bother asking me. I know that sounds harsh and weird, but it's the way it is. And if you can't deal with that, with the way things are … the way *I* am, then it's fine. I totally understand, and I won't take it personally. We can still be friends—if you want to be, of course," I'm quick to add.

Silence hits the room. The weight of my words settles into the distance between us.

"Audrey … I can't be friends with you."

Ouch.

I was expecting it, but it still hurts.

"It's fine. I totally get it." My eyes start searching out the location of my sweater. I need to cover up. Which is stupid because it's not like I'm actually naked right now. If I were, then we wouldn't be having this conversation.

"No, you don't." The firmness of his tone brings my eyes straight back to his. "I can't be friends with you, Audrey. Because it wouldn't be possible. Not with the way I feel when I'm around you. Fuck. It's been a struggle this far, not to touch you … kiss you. So, no, I'm not doing it again. You have something you can't share with me? Fine. I accept that. Because honestly, Audrey, I will take you any way I can have you."

My heart is in my throat, trapped there along with any words I might say.

All I can do is stare at him. My chest heaving up and down.

I'm not sure who moves first. Him. Me. Who really cares?

All I do know is that we crash back into each other. I'm in his arms. Our lips devouring. Hands roaming. Bodies melding.

Jack and I seem to have two speeds only. Zero and sixty. We jump from one to the other in the blink of an eye.

But I'm determined that we stay in the fast lane until zero is our only option because we're both too blissed out to move.

I've never had this type of passion with anyone ever. Sure, I've had lusty sex in my past. But nothing like what I'm feeling right now with Jack.

I want him with the kind of hunger that could starve a whole goddamn city.

Jack carries me through to my bedroom. He sets me down on the edge of the bed and comes down to his knees in front of me.

Reaching for my bedside lamp, I turn it on, wanting to see him.

The light glows off the golden skin of his chest. His eyes look so incredibly blue right now.

"You're stunning," I tell him.

He cups my cheek with his hand. "*You're* stunning," he says, voice raspy.

I feel shy all of a sudden, my face heating.

Jack rests back on his haunches and takes hold of one of my legs. Lifting it, he pulls my boot off and then my sock. He does the same with the other foot.

His eyes meet back with mine.

Then, his fingers begin unfastening my jeans.

Pressing my hands to the bed, I raise my hips to allow him to remove them.

He peels the jeans down my legs, leaving me in my panties.

They're black and lacy.

I might have put a pair of my sexy, old-life-Audrey undies on—you know, just in case this moment with Jack did arise. I might have shaved every square inch of my body too.

"Jesus," he breathes. His eyes fixed on the spot between my legs.

His hand runs up my smooth leg, reaching the top of my thigh. His fingers trace an invisible line to where I need him most. The tips of his fingers only just touching the edge of my panties.

My body starts to shiver with need.

Jack looks at me, and the expression in his eyes is ... undiluted lust.

No one has ever looked at me in such a way before. I feel like, right now, the only thing he sees is me.

"I know ... this stays ..." His fingers give a light tug on the hem on my tank.

Immediately, embarrassment and shame start to cover me.

"Don't."

I give him a confused look. "Don't what?" I whisper.

"Be self-conscious or whatever the fuck it is you're feeling right now. It's me, Audrey. You never have to feel either of those things with me. I just need to know the boundaries. Where I can and can't touch you."

I lick my dry lips, swallowing. "You can ... touch me everywhere ... just not here." I press my hand to the marred section of skin that sits beneath my breasts and above my belly button.

"Okay." He nods. "So, the boobs are mine."

The glint in his eyes has my own lips tugging upward.

"All yours." And to prove the point, I unsnap my bra through my tank. Pull the straps down my arms and tug it free from its confines.

Jack leans forward and presses a kiss to my mouth. Then, he moves down, planting a kiss in the center of my chest.

His hand comes up, cupping my breast through my tank. The contact is amazing. But I wish I could feel his skin on me.

He rubs his thumb over my nipple, and I shudder.

His mouth finds mine. With a sweep of his tongue, his teeth graze over my bottom lip.

"I want to see you here." He gives a gentle squeeze of my boob. "I want to touch you here. Kiss you here."

I want that too, but …

"I'm going to pull your tank down a little, so I can kiss you there. I won't go any lower than there." His finger draws a line down between my breasts, making me shiver.

My heart starts to pound in my chest as he begins to kiss a path down to my breasts.

When his fingers curl over the fabric of my tank and he lowers it slowly, carefully, my body starts trembling.

"Is this too much, too soon?" He presses a kiss to the swell of my breast.

I shake my head. "Just … don't go too far."

"You can trust me," he says, and I believe him.

In this moment, I trust Jack with me, and I never thought I would be able to say that ever again.

The revelation is startling to me.

Jack lowers the fabric of my tank until he reveals my nipple. He groans a low, erotic sound that vibrates all the way down to my core.

"So fucking pretty," he murmurs and then closes his lips around my nipple.

A hot gasp escapes me. My hands immediately go to his head, clutching him to me.

It feels insanely good. And it's been forever since any man touched me skin to skin here.

Jack swirls his tongue around my nipple, teeth skimming the hardened point of it, while he makes quick work of freeing the other breast, cupping it in his hand.

My tank sits beneath my breasts, covering what he can never see but giving him the access we both so desperately need.

Jack licks and sucks each breast, driving me to the point of crazy.

My hips are restless, searching him out.

When I feel his hand move between my legs, I almost come apart right then and there.

Fingers slide inside the fabric, slipping easily between my folds because I'm embarrassingly wet for him.

"Jesus," Jack groans. "You're soaked."

He slides a finger inside me, and it's my turn to moan.

His finger retreats as quickly as it arrived, and I whimper at the loss.

"Don't worry," he croons. "I got you."

He slides my panties off, getting the last barrier out of the way.

"Spread your legs wide for me, Audrey."

I shamelessly do as he asked, widening them for him. Opening myself up for him.

I'm not a bare-down-there kind of girl. I have a neatly trimmed landing strip, which he seems to appreciate, if his heated expression is anything to go by.

"Sexy as fuck," he rumbles.

I watch him as he runs a finger down between my lips, and then with a deliberate slowness, he pushes it back inside of me.

The desire in his eyes is an aphrodisiac in itself. Seeing the way his bright eyes darken with desire over me is my new favorite thing.

"Need to taste you," he growls, and then he covers my pussy with his mouth.

Jesus.

I cry out at the feel of his hot mouth on my most sensitive part.

I can't remember the last time a man did this to me.

Maybe that's because they never did it the way Jack is. It's like he knows exactly how and where to touch me.

His tongue swirls my clit with just the right amount of pressure. While his finger makes good work inside me, fucking me.

Watching his head move between my legs is incredibly erotic. I want to take a photo, just for spank-bank purposes alone.

It's not long before I feel the telltale signs of an impending orgasm. My legs start to tingle.

It's quick, but honestly, I'm not surprised.

It has been a long time since I came by anything other than my own hand.

"Jack …" I breathe his name like a prayer.

"That's it. Come for me." His muffled words against my clit are my undoing.

It hits me with the force of a tornado. Picking me up and tossing me around. My whole body shaking from the intensity of it.

And it is a hell of a long time before I come back down to earth.

I'm sprawled on the bed, unable to hold myself up.

My eyes move down to Jack, who is still sitting between my legs. His mouth glistens with my desire for him.

I watch, enraptured, as he runs his tongue around his lips, tasting the last of me.

I swear I come again just from seeing that.

"So incredibly fucking hot."

He kicks off his boots. His hands go to his jeans, and he shoves them down his legs. His eyes not leaving me once.

But mine stray the exact moment he removes his boxer shorts.

"Jesus," I whisper at the sight of his long, thick erection straining upward.

"Not his. Mine." He smirks.

My mind goes back to our earlier conversation, and I bite my lip, teasing, "Ready to show me the non-gentlemanly side of you in bed?"

His head tilts to the side. "Haven't I done that already?"

"I know you've been holding back a little ... being careful with me. Because ..." My eyes lower, but I won't screw up this moment because of my issues. Taking a deep breath, I look back to him. "But don't hold back. Please. I want you to give me everything. Show me ... *every* ungentlemanly way you can *fuck*."

Eyes flaring, he tears open a condom packet that I didn't even know he was holding and rolls the rubber onto his dick.

"I was going to drag this out," he tells me. "Make it last. Do it sweet and slow. But then you went and said those sexy-ass words to me ..." He's holding his cock in his hand, fist squeezing it.

My eyes are fixed there as I hang on to every single word he's saying to me.

"Come *here*." He punctuates the word like an order.

And I race to obey, clambering off the bed with the speed of a racehorse. I would be embarrassed if I wasn't so desperate for him.

"Kiss me," he tells me in a low voice.

I reach up onto my tiptoes and press my mouth to his, softly kissing him, sucking his lower lip.

Then, I replace my mouth with my fingers, tracing the wetness I just put on his lips.

I slip my finger into his mouth. He catches it with his teeth, and my insides clench.

I reach my other hand out and touch the tip of his cock, sliding my fingers over his. Jack removes his hand, and I cover his cock with my own.

I start stroking him up and down.

His eyes darken, and I see the exact moment when his control snaps.

He lifts me. My back hits the wall. And he thrusts up inside me.

"Yes!" I cry out at the welcome invasion.

"Jesus … Audrey," Jack groans. "You're so fucking tight."

"It's been a while," I confess.

His eyes meet with mine. He grins. "Lucky me then."

And he starts to fuck me. Hard. Pounding me into the wall. His tongue thrusting inside my mouth.

There is no finesse here.

Just lust.

I'm almost frantic with desire.

And I'm not alone in this. Jack is in high gear, like I am.

We're like addicts getting our fix from each other's bodies.

And I am here for every single drop of what he has to give me.

The sounds of our heavy breaths, skin slapping skin, fill the room.

It's pure, carnal fucking.

Then, I'm on my feet. Turning. Palms put against the wall. Hips pulled back.

"Spread those gorgeous legs for me, Audrey."

I widen my stance and glance back over my shoulder at him through the curtain of my messed up hair.

Jack's smile is all foxlike.

Then, he slides his cock back inside me, and my eyes roll into my head.

His hands cover mine, holding them to the wall, and he starts fucking me again. Hips pumping in and out. Faster and faster.

Until I'm breathless. Sweat dripping from my body.

And as I quickly learn, Jack is a mover.

His sex positions last for no longer than a few minutes at a time before he switches them up, shifting me around like I weigh no more than air.

And the fact that he can go for way longer than a few minutes is every girl's wet dream come true.

He screws me all over my bedroom. My ass and back touch almost every surface in here. Who knew having sex against a window was even a thing? Thank God the curtains are closed, so no one outside can see my bare ass pressed up against it.

Jack wasn't kidding when he said he wasn't a gentleman in the bedroom.

He has the moves and stamina of a porn star on Viagra.

He's not selfish though. He makes sure I get mine. That I feel every drop of pleasure that he's giving to me.

Jack is literally screwing every bad memory out of my head.

For this blissful moment in time, I am nothing but an empty mind and an overstimulated body. Being screwed into oblivion by the most beautiful man I have ever laid my eyes on.

I can regret it all tomorrow.

But now ... now, I am going to enjoy every hot, euphoric second of it.

I have honestly never had sex like this in my life.

If I thought I had been fucked before ...

I was wrong.

So very wrong.

This right here is fucking.

It's primitive, headboard-banging sex with an alpha male.

We're on the bed now. I'm flat on my back. Jack is on top of me. My legs are wrapped around him while he pumps in and out of me.

We're burning up the sheets, the bed ... my whole goddamn apartment.

My legs start to tingle. My orgasm quickly building.

But I'm not ready to come yet. I don't want this to be over.

It's been going for ... I have no clue. All I do know is that it's been a hell of a long time.

And still, I don't want it to end. I don't want my one promised night with Jack to be over.

Not yet.

I try to pull my hips back, needing to ease the contact for a second.

Jack chases me back down. "Don't fight it. Come for me."

"But I'm not ready for it to end." I'm practically sobbing.

I don't want this to ever stop. I want to live in this moment with him forever.

He grasps hold of my chin, forcing my eyes on his. "It won't end. Because I'm nowhere near done with you." He presses his hips into mine, kissing me. "Now, come for me."

He takes both of my hands up over my head, pinning them down.

His head drops down. Lips capturing my nipple, he sucks hard as he gives one good, firm thrust, and I couldn't stop the orgasm even if I tried.

I scream out his name. My pussy clamping around his dick like a vise. Every muscle in my body seizing.

I'm coming so long and hard that I almost black out.

"Jesus," Jack hisses. He grabs a handful of my sweat-soaked hair. "I'm gonna … fucking … come." His mouth kisses mine hard, biting and licking, his hips snapping against mine.

And then he comes.

And keeps coming.

Jack's ragged groan reverberates through me, like a shot of adrenaline to the veins.

He drops his face into my neck, breathing fast.

I'm struggling to catch my own breath. And find my lost sanity.

It's on my floor somewhere—along with my panties.

We lie there together, coming down from our high.

I expect to feel regret. Like I did when he made me come yesterday.

But I don't.

Jack is still buried deep inside me.

His scent and skin all over me.

All I feel in this moment is … sated. Yet unsated too.

Like I haven't gotten quite enough of him.

I've had a taste, and now, I want more.

Hellfire.

Jack lifts his head and looks at me. His waves fall onto his forehead.

"Hi." He smiles.

I brush his hair aside with my fingers. "Hi."

I feel shy. Which is pretty wild, considering I just let him screw me to kingdom come and back.

"That was …"

"Like nothing you've had before," he finishes for me, a grin in his eyes.

"I was going to say, good. But we can up it to great, if that makes you feel better."

"Ouch." He chuckles, and the sound is easy. It makes me warm in a way the sex never could.

He brushes his lips over mine. "Well, you're like nothing I've ever known before, pretty girl. And that … that was some fucking out-of-this-world kind of sex."

"So, you thought it was good too?"

He laughs again.

I love that it's me making him laugh.

And I'm choosing not to examine what that means exactly.

"Let me get rid of the condom."

He lifts up, pulling out of me. The emptiness I feel when he's no longer inside of me is more pronounced than I want it to be.

I sit up as Jack does, ready to swing my legs over the edge of the bed.

He stops moving. "Where are you going?"

"To get my panties."

He climbs over me, forcing me onto my back. He hovers over me on his hands, hair framing his face. "And why do you need them?"

"Um ... because we're finished having sex."

"No."

"No what?"

"No, we're not finished having sex. Not by a long shot. I ain't done with you yet, Audrey."

Holy bananas.

"And what if I'm done with you?" I'm totally not done with him either, but I am suddenly in the mood to tease.

His brow rises. "Then, you'd be making a mistake. That there, what we just did? That was the starter. We haven't even gotten to the main course yet."

Holy. Fucking. Sex. Drive.

"That wasn't ... are you a machine?" I ask in all seriousness.

He laughs. His smile all fox. "No. I just have a high sex drive, and I can go all night." He leans down and brushes a kiss over my lips, making me shiver. "And I plan on spending those hours exploring every inch of your gorgeous body with my tongue and fingers and making you come again with both. And then, when I'm done with that, I'll be putting my cock in more than one of your holes." He kisses me again, sucking on my bottom lip, indicating exactly where he plans on putting his dick.

And I am all here for that. But I am still in the mood to play.

I lift a brow. "And what if I don't like sucking dick?"

Jack laughs softly. "Then, I'll just have to keep putting it in my favorite hole. Again and again and … again." He slips a hand between my legs.

I'm already soaked from his words alone.

We both groan at the contact.

"Jesus, Audrey. You ain't going anywhere." He moves his finger over my clit, teasing.

And I nod my head in agreement.

He pushes his finger inside me, and I close my eyes, basking in the feeling. Right where I need him to be.

"We're going to be doing this all night."

"Yes," I pant as he starts moving his finger in and out of me.

I've lost my mind to him. Caring about that fact at this moment in time isn't even an option.

Then, he pulls his finger out of me, pushing up to his knees.

I stare at him, disappointed at the loss of him.

He removes the condom. It's not something I have ever thought of as hot before. But as I watch Jack do it, knowing what's about to come—hopefully, me again and very soon—well, hell, it's the sexiest thing ever.

He throws the condom in the waste bin. Taking himself in his hand, he starts slowly jacking himself off in front of me.

Sweet Lawd.

I sit up and wrap my hand around his, taking over, like I did earlier. But only this time, I plan on doing more. So much more.

"Fuck yeah. That's it, just like that," he tells me in that raspy voice of his.

I innocently blink up at him and lick my lips. "Oh, and just so you know … what I said before, I was lying. I do like sucking dick."

The sound of his groan as my head descends, taking his dick in my mouth, is almost my own undoing.

A girl could come alone from just listening to that desire-fueled groan.

He tastes like sex and latex. And I'm not hating it either.

Weird.

But it's hard not to like anything about Jack.

I work him over with my lips and tongue, bringing out my A game.

He's big though, and I have never been a deep-throat kind of girl. So, the rest of him that I can't fit into my mouth, I jack off with my hand.

"Jesus, Audrey. You suck me so good." His hands grip my head, and he starts thrusting into my mouth. But he isn't a jerk about it. He seems to know my limits. "Fuck, I need to stop, or I'll come in your mouth."

He pulls away. I try to chase him back, wanting him to come in my mouth, wanting to taste him, but he's not having it.

Next thing I know, I'm on my back, my legs up in the air with his arms hooked around them, holding me in place.

I stare up at him. "I wanted you to come in my mouth." I pout.

His eyes darken, and he growls a sexy sound. "Later. But right now, it's my turn to taste you again."

TWENTY

We're lying on our backs, next to each other, after that last round of sex. Both panting and soaked with sweat. My tank is drenched through and stuck to my body.

I am actually starting to think that Jack is a robot.

A legit, real robot.

I've never known a guy who could go for that long or that much.

I thought it was only in myths and pornos.

Seems it happens in real life too.

I'm not quite sure I deserve it. Deserve him. All gorgeous, six-foot-three fucking machine of him.

But I'm not going to look this gift horse in the mouth either. I might be stupid, but I'm not totally dumb.

I promised myself one night with Jack, and I plan on making the absolute most of it.

Even if that means I'll be walking tomorrow like I've got saddle sore.

It will be totally worth it.

"Are you real?" I turn my head to look at him.

He's smiling. "I'm not sure how to answer that question."

I shift onto my side, placing my hand under my head to support it. "Your stamina is unreal."

He laughs.

"I'm serious." I press my hand to his damp chest. "It's inhuman. Are you a machine or something?"

He's still laughing, louder now. He moves onto his side, putting us face-to-face. "You're good for a man's ego."

"And you're good for a woman's orgasm count." I grin.

His hand lands on my thigh. He lifts it, hooking it over his leg, bringing me closer to him.

I like that he needs me near. I like it a whole lot.

"And we've only just gotten started." He kisses me once, softly, gently.

So out of context with the way he just spent the last …

Actually, what the hell time is it?

My eyes seek out the alarm clock on my nightstand. *Jesus. It's late.*

"Do you need to go back to your apartment?"

"Do you want me to go back to my apartment?"

"Stop answering a question with a question." I lightly bat at his chest, and he chuckles. "I'm not kicking you out. I was just wondering if Eleven needed to be fed."

"I put her food down before I left for our date, so she's good."

"She won't break out again?"

"It's always a possibility."

"You can … bring her over here, if you want to …"

He stares back at me. "Are you asking me to stay the night?"

Looking away, I shrug and bite my lip.

I do want him to stay. But I'm afraid to admit it to myself as much as I'm afraid to admit it to him.

His finger curls under my chin, and his thumb tugs my lip free.

"Well, if you were asking me to get my pussy and stay over tonight, then my answer would most definitely be yes."

Laughter splutters from me. "Your pussy?"

His brow rises, but I can see the humor in his eyes. "Cat. You pervert."

"Uh-huh. I'm the pervert," I tease. "You're the one who brought up pussies."

"I like pussies. They're my favorite."

I'm laughing harder now. I can't remember the last time I laughed like this. "No kidding."

He gently pushes me onto my back. Climbing over me, his hips between mine, he holds himself up on his hands and stares down at me.

"What?" I ask, smiling up at him.

"I like it when you laugh. A fuck of a lot. Your whole face lights up, and you get this glow about you. You are always beautiful, Audrey. But when you laugh, you are on a whole other level."

My heart feels like it's stopped beating. Like time has ceased moving.

That's literally *the* nicest thing anyone has ever said to me. I honestly have no words.

All I can do is stare at him.

I reach a hand to his face. I brush my fingers over his forehead, down his temple, along his cheekbone, loving the way his eyes close at my touch.

I place my hand to his cheek and guide his mouth down to mine as I lift my head up to meet him halfway.

"Ask me," he whispers right before our lips touch.

"What?"

"You know what."

He wants me to ask him to stay over.

Why is this such a big deal for me to say? It's not like I'm asking the guy to marry me.

Taking a breath, I shove my nerves away and whisper, "Stay the night."

He presses his lips to mine, softly kissing me. "My answer will always be yes."

I can't help but smile against his mouth.

Then, he gives me one more lasting peck on the lips and pushes off me, getting up from the bed. "I'll go get Eleven and bring her back here. I'll be five minutes, max."

I watch Jack as he pulls on his jeans and pushes his feet into his boots.

"Your sweater's in the living room," I tell him, biting my lip at the memory of him removing it.

Jack grins, and then he leans down and gives me another kiss before he exits my bedroom. I hear the click of the front door opening and shutting a second later.

I flop back on my bed, letting out a giggle, covering my face with my hands.

I can't believe I just had sex with Jack.

Multiple times!

Oh. My. Sweet. God!

He's so frigging hot.

And I can't stop smiling.

I have just broken every single rule in my own damn book, and I don't care.

Because, you know … orgasms.

I know I should have ended the night just then. Not asked him to stay over.

But truth be told … I want him here.

And it's not just the sex. Although that is awesome.

It's having him here. Talking to him. Listening to him talk to me. Having that physical closeness with another human being.

Just to have one night when I'm not alone and afraid.

And being with Jack, it's so much more than I imagined it could be.

It has been so long since I had anything near to what I've had tonight.

Well, honestly, I have never had anything like what I have just experienced with Jack.

To say the sex was phenomenal would be a severe understatement.

The man's stamina is insane. I didn't know if I was going to be able to keep up with him at one point. Thank God he mostly took the lead.

How the guy is currently single is shocking to me.

How his girlfriend managed to let him go is beyond me.

He's gorgeous, and he screws like a porn star.

My girl parts are tingling just at the thought of the things he did to me. The things we did together.

The soreness between my legs is a constant reminder of having him there.

How can I feel as empty as I do without him here right now?

I actually miss him. He only went over to his apartment and will be back soon, and I'm lying here like a damn sap, missing him.

Which is pathetic.

But true.

I'm acting ridiculous.

God, get a grip, Audrey.

Scrubbing my hands over my face, I let out something between a laugh and a wistful sigh before I clamber out of bed.

Obviously, I still have my tank on. Which is damp from all the physical exertion Jack just put me through.

But my boobs are hanging out the top.

Classy.

Chuckling to myself, I pull my tank back up, covering the girls.

Jack seems to be a breast man. And an ass man. He also seems to like spending a considerable amount of time between my legs.

Not that I'm complaining. Never, ever would I complain about that.

I giggle again to myself.

Listen to me, giggling like a little schoolgirl. I need to sort myself out.

I grab a fresh tank top and a pair of pajama shorts out of my drawer. My back is to the bedroom door, and I know Jack's not back yet because I would have heard the front door open, but even still, I glance over my shoulder, making sure I'm alone.

I quickly tug off my damp tank top and change into the new one, covering myself back up. I toss the dirty one in the laundry hamper and pull on the pajama shorts.

Then, I use the bathroom, giving my teeth a quick scrub clean, and then pad my way through to the kitchen to get a glass of water.

I've just finished filling up my glass when my apartment door opens, and Jack walks through with Eleven in his arms.

I can't help the smile that spreads across my face. My body lighting back up for him.

It's crazy.

The moment Eleven sees me, she jumps down from Jack's arms and comes trotting over to me. She hops up onto the kitchen counter, and I can't even tell her to get down because it's so damn cute how happy she is to see me.

I stroke her fur, and she purrs happily, wandering up and down the counter, winding her tail around my arm.

After turning one of the dead bolts, Jack walks over, coming up behind me. He wraps his arms around my waist. "Someone missed you."

"I missed her."

He presses a kiss to my temple. "And I missed you."

I laugh softly. No way am I admitting I missed him too. I'm not that weak for him. Yet. "You were gone five minutes," I whisper, sliding my hands over his.

He places his lips on the juncture between my neck and shoulder. "Five minutes too long away from you. And you." His hand glides down my belly to cup between my legs.

I turn in his arms, bringing us face-to-face. Well, my face to his chest. He's so much taller than me.

I rest my face against his chest. I can smell myself on his skin, and something primal and possessive passes through me.

Lifting my head, I push up onto my toes and press my mouth to his.

Jack makes this sexy, growly sound. Then, he picks me up, sets me on the counter, and stands between my legs.

I hook my ankles together around him, holding him to me. Not that he seems keen to go anywhere.

He presses his face to my neck, running his nose along my pulse point, inhaling. "I like smelling me on you."

His teeth graze along my jaw, making me shiver.

"I like having you on me, period."

I feel his smile against my skin.

"And how about *in* you, pretty girl? You like that too?"

"I think you already know the answer to that, soldier." I dig my heels into his ass, making my point.

He nips my bottom lip with his teeth before fitting his mouth over mine.

I moan into the kiss, my fingers winding into his hair.

"Fuck. You taste good," he breathes.

"I brushed my teeth."

He chuckles. "I didn't mean the mint. Although that's nice too."

He takes another kiss from my lips before moving down my neck, trailing kisses to my collarbone. I tip my head back to give him better access. A hand covers my breast, squeezing, causing a bolt of lust to shoot straight between my legs.

Needing contact, I press myself against him. He's hard already.

Knowing I do that to him only turns me on further.

Jack licks a path back to my mouth. His hands find my hips, and he tugs me even tighter to his body.

We're hip to hip. Chest to chest. Mouth to mouth.

The only way we could be closer is if he were inside me. And knowing that is happening real soon just drives my need for him higher.

Jack circles his hips, rubbing his denim-covered erection against me. Creating a delicious friction through my pajama bottoms.

I can feel how wet I am. I'm soaking through my shorts, likely leaving a wet patch on Jack's jeans, and I can't even care to be embarrassed because it feels so damn good.

I tug Jack's shirt up, needing to see him. He removes it in that sexy way he does.

How can the way he takes off his shirt turn me on?

No clue. But it does.

I glide my fingers over his abs, up to his nipples, running my fingers over one, testing his sensitivity there.

By the way his blue eyes flare, he seems to like it. A lot.

I dip my head and kiss his chest, licking my way over one nipple.

A growl rumbles beneath his skin. I feel the effect of it against my lips.

He grabs my head, bringing my mouth back to his, and plunders it with his tongue. Practically fucking my mouth.

Another erogenous zone found.

Win for Audrey.

Grabbing my legs, he pulls them from around his body. His hands make fast work of removing my pajama shorts.

"Jesus," he growls when he sees that I'm not wearing panties, making me smile. "And I thought the sight of you in those panties earlier was hot. This is so much better."

He brings my shorts to his face, pressing his nose into them, and inhales.

Sweet Christ on a cracker.

That is so freaking sexy.

Dropping the shorts to the floor, he unfastens his jeans. The lowering of the zip is erotically loud in the silence of my apartment.

He pushes them down, and his cock springs free from its confines.

It stands hard and proud against his stomach.

My mouth actually waters at the sight, knowing exactly how it tastes and feels when my lips are wrapped around his dick.

"Going commando too?" I bite my lower lip, watching him from beneath my lashes.

"Anything to aid quicker access to fucking you."

His bold openness in regard to sex is like crack for me. I love it when he talks this way.

He kicks his jeans off, and then he is magnificently naked in front of me.

My hands curl around the edge of the counter. It is all I can do to keep me there and stop myself from launching at him like a sex-depraved nympho.

Jack steps closer to me. His hands wrap around my feet, and he lifts them up, setting my heels on the countertop.

I'm wide open and exposed to him.

"I fucking love how wet you get for me." He dips his finger between my folds, dragging it over my clit, making me shudder.

I shouldn't be this turned on.

I've already had more orgasms in the past few hours than I've had in the last few years.

But even still, my body is crying out for more.

For more of him.

I wonder if I will ever get my fill.

Part of me hopes not. The stupid part of me, that is.

Jack's eyes are fixed where his hand is. "Need to taste you again," he rumbles. He drops to his knees on my kitchen floor and buries his face against my pussy.

"Oh God," I moan, grabbing hold of his hair.

He runs his nose up and down, getting my wetness on his skin.

It's incredibly erotic. But then so is everything else that he does to me.

His hands move between my legs, fingers opening my folds, exposing my most sensitive parts to him.

"So fucking pretty."

The tip of his tongue licks my clit. It's scorching hot. Like every single part of me.

Then, he blows a stream of cool air over my clit.

He repeats this over and over, driving me crazy.

"Jack," I whine. Needing more. More pressure. More him. More everything.

His eyes lift to mine. The grin on his face is unrepentant. The bastard is enjoying teasing me.

"You need this?" He leisurely slides a finger inside me.

"Yes," I hiss. "God, yes."

He starts slowly fucking me with his thick finger.

In and out.

Then, he puts his mouth back on me. With his finger buried deep inside me, he does a come-hither motion, hitting the sweetest of all spots. One I didn't even know existed until this very moment.

Then, he sucks my clit into his mouth.

And I go off like a firecracker.

I didn't even see the orgasm coming.

It hits me like the g-force on a roller coaster.

My hips pump against his face, riding the orgasm out until I'm weak and boneless.

But Jack isn't finished. He's still licking and sucking, like he can't get enough of me.

"Jack," I pant. "I can't."

"Yes," he growls against my pussy, "you can." He removes his finger, replacing it with his tongue, fucking me with it, while his thumb now rubs over my clit. Back and forth. In and out.

"Fuck," I whimper, falling back onto my elbows, no longer able to keep myself up.

It's barely seconds before I feel myself starting to climb to the peak again.

Seems Jack knows my body better than I do.

Because I come there again, minutes later, with Jack's tongue buried deep inside me.

I'm panting, gasping for air. Limp like a noodle. Shamelessly splayed out on my kitchen countertop.

Jack gets to his feet. His hair is pulled in every direction from my gripping hands. His face glistening with my cum.

He wipes the back of his hand over his mouth.

"You're so fucking hot," I tell him.

He likes that because his eyes darken with lust. "Need you," he rasps.

"Take me."

He grabs a condom from the pocket of his jeans and tears the foil open, rolling the rubber onto his engorged cock.

I move to drop my feet from the counter and sit up, but Jack catches hold of them, shaking his head.

"Stay put."

I lower my back down to the cool surface. It feels good against my overheated skin.

Hands still gripping my feet, Jack lifts my legs. Turning his head to one, he licks a path up the arch of my foot.

Holy hell.

My whole body is trembling and shuddering.

"You like that?" he asks.

All I can do is nod.

He repeats the motion again on my other foot before placing my legs over his shoulders.

Taking his cock in hand, he rubs it between my folds.

Pausing it at my entrance, he stares into my eyes, and then he starts to slowly bury himself to the hilt.

My eyes pretty much roll back into my head when he hits home.

It's like feeling him for the first time all over again.

I wonder if I will ever get used to taking Jack inside of me and the feelings it gives me … that he gives me.

Part of me hopes I never do.

One of his strong arms wraps across both my thighs, pulling my hips to the edge of the counter.

Then, bracing his hands on either side of my head, Jack starts to fuck me.

There is no tenderness in this. Just like the other times he screwed me.

It's a good, old-fashioned, lust-fueled fucking.

He's jackhammering in and out of me.

My breasts bounce beneath my tank top.

I wish that I could take this top off, let Jack see them … me … fully.

But I can't, and I'm not even going to wish for more when I have this right here.

Him, right here with me. Giving me everything he has to give.

"Fuck, Audrey. I love how incredible your pussy feels. Tight like a fist."

"Around your big dick," I add.

I surprise myself, saying it. I like hearing dirty talk, but I don't usually say those things myself. I'm not really a vocal person in bed. Jack is a talker, and I really do love it. It is such a massive turn-on.

Jack growls, his mouth coming to cover mine as he keeps on fucking me. My breasts crushed to his chest, I drag my nails down his back.

And he fucks me harder and harder.

"Getting close, Audrey. Need you there with me."

"Yes," I chant. "Yes."

And I'm not lying. There is no need for faking with Jack. Because he gets me there every single time.

No matter how many orgasms he's already given me, my body seems to be primed and ready to go again for him at any given moment.

I feel the impending signs of my orgasm.

"Come now, Audrey. I can't hold off much longer."

"I'm almost … there …" I pant. "Jack!" I grip his waist, digging my nails into his skin, as I explode around his cock.

I feel him start to come immediately, his dick pulsing fiercely inside of me.

He wasn't kidding when he said he was close.

I love that he holds off on coming, waiting for me. Needing us to come together.

It's sweet. And hot.

So very goddamn hot.

His forehead is pressed to mine. Both of us trying to catch our breaths.

"That was … amazing," I say when I've finally gotten control of my breathing.

"*You're* amazing." He pushes my hair back off my sweat-dampened forehead and presses a tender kiss to my cheek and then another to my lips.

"As are you." I stifle a sudden yawn.

"You tired?" Jack asks.

"You've worn me out."

That makes him smile.

"Need a shower though. I'm all sticky."

"Same."

Jack lifts himself up, bringing me with him.

He holds me against him for a moment.

His hand in my hair, the other wrapped around my back, he hugs me.

Emotion packs itself into my chest.

I hug Jack back, listening to the beat of his strong heart.

He presses a kiss to the top of my head and then pulls back.

I really don't like the feeling when he's no longer inside me.

I feel empty. Alone.

Like I was for so long before he came into my life.

Jack helps me down from the counter, and then he removes his condom, ties it off, and gets rid of it in the wastebasket.

Leaving Jack, I head to the bathroom and take a shower. Washing my hair and cleaning my body. I don't like removing the scent of him from me, but knowing he's waiting out there for me makes it all the better.

When I'm finished, Jack gets in the shower after me.

I dress quickly while he's in the shower, putting on another fresh tank top and going with just panties this time.

I'm brushing out the tangles in my hair when Jack comes out of the bathroom in just a towel.

"Hey." I smile at the sight of him.

I put my hairbrush down and climb into bed, getting under the covers.

Jack dries off before going back into the bathroom to take the towel back, and I happily watch his naked butt retreat away.

He turns the light off when he returns, still very much naked. And if I'm not wrong, he's rocking a semi.

He gets into bed beside me, lying on his back, pulling me into his arms. I rest my head on his chest, my fingers playing with the line of hair that runs from his belly button to one of my favorite parts of his body.

"Jack?"

"Hmm?"

"Is your cock hard again?"

I hear and feel his deep chuckle.

"You're seriously ready for round ... what are we at now?" I ask, stunned at this man's ability to get a boner.

"No clue. I lost count," he admits, and we both laugh this time. "And to answer your question, yeah, my dick is hard again."

I turn my eyes up to his. "Is it always like that—permanently rocking a semi?"

A grin reaches his eyes. "Only since I met you. I've been hard every day since."

Well, if that doesn't boost my ego.

"I've been wet every day since I met you."

It only seems fair to share that information with him.

"Fucking hell," he growls. "Keep saying stuff like that, and there'll be no sleep for either of us tonight."

I smile, unrepentant. "Is that a promise?"

"You can bet your sweet ass it is."

"Then, you should probably also know that I've masturbated to thoughts of you pretty much every night since I met you too."

He moves so fast that I barely get a chance to blink before I'm on my back and he's on top of me, hips between my legs.

"Just for that teasing, you're going to do that for me right now."

"What?"

"Masturbate in front of me. I want to see you get yourself off."

I feel myself flush all over. But I'm not opposed to the thought either.

Honestly, I really like the thought of doing that for him.

"Fair enough. But only if you do the same."

"You want to see me jerk off, Audrey?"

I bite my lip and nod my head. I can feel heat rising in my cheeks, flooding down my chest, over my breasts, covering my body.

"You want me to show you what I do every night in bed and every morning in the shower with the thought of only you in my head?"

He's masturbated over me too? It's another boost to my ego.

"All these weeks I've spent jerking over you. Lot of wasted time really, when we could have been doing this ... doing each other. So, let's not waste any more time, huh? Let's make up for the time we lost instead."

And we do.

Neither of us gets a wink of sleep until we're boneless and exhausted in the early hours of the morning.

And it isn't until that moment, when I'm on the cusp of sleep, lying in the comfort of Jack's arms, that I realize I never did the usual sweep of my apartment when I first got home. I was too busy falling into Jack to even give it a second thought.

And the locks on my front door ...

I didn't bolt them all up.

Just one lock is keeping my door secure.

And ... I don't feel scared.

I feel safe.

Because of Jack.

TWENTY-ONE

I open my eyes to find Jack already awake and watching me.

"Morning." I smile. My voice is croaky.

"Morning." He leans close and brushes a soft kiss over my lips.

I try not to breathe on him, consciously aware of my morning breath.

I snuggle against his warm chest. He wraps his arms around me.

"How long have you been awake?" I ask him.

"Not long."

"Did you sleep okay?"

"Better than I have in a long time."

That makes me smile.

It's also the same for me. I can't remember the last time I slept so easily.

I feel well rested.

I always sleep on high alert nowadays. I sleep light, ready to hear any noise that shouldn't be there. And if I ever do drop into a deep sleep, it's plagued with nightmares and bad memories.

But this morning, I feel lighter. Almost like I had a dreamless sleep.

It's crazy how one person can come into your life and change things for the better in the smallest period of time. I refuse to think about how a person can do the exact opposite in limited time too.

My past is over and done with.

This is the here and now, and as I lie here, staring into Jack's gorgeous eyes, things look a whole lot brighter.

"What time is it?" I yawn.

"Just after eight."

I groan. "Ugh."

"Do you have to work today?"

"Yeah. I start work in an hour."

"I'll drive you in."

"You don't have to." I look up at him.

"If I don't, you'll walk, right? That means, you'll have to leave earlier, and that means, I'll have less time with you. Also, I need to work on my book. Where better than the library? It's quiet, and the view is fantastic there."

His hand squeezes my ass cheek, making me giggle.

I'm giggling all the damn time around him.

It's hideous.

I really need to stop it.

"We can have lunch together, if you want?"

"Oh, well, I was going to go into the adoption center today on my lunch break and sign up for more dog-walking."

He smiles. I can tell he likes that.

"Any dog in particular?" he asks.

"Gary." I grin. "I feel bad for Pork Chop though. But I don't think I'm strong enough to walk him when he pulls."

"So, why don't I join you? We can walk them together."

"Another date?" I ask, my eyes searching his.

He stares into my eyes. "You can call it another date. I'll just call it dating." He presses a soft, sweet kiss to my lips. "Which is what we're doing, if you didn't know."

"We are?"

"Uh-huh."

"Do I get a say in this?"

"Of course you do. You'll say we shouldn't date. But give me no actual solid reason as to why. I'll counterargue that you're being stupid because, clearly, we should be dating—if not for the chemistry between us alone. We'll bicker back and forth. I'll lose patience, and I'll shut you up with a kiss. That will undoubtedly turn into sex. You'll have a minimum of two orgasms— which is great. But then you will be late for work—not so great. Ultimately, you'll give in and admit what we both know is inevitable for you and me, Audrey ... which is, yes, we are dating."

My mouth is hanging open in shock.

"Or"—he presses a kiss to my open lips—"you can just agree with what we both know is inevitable—that we should be a couple. And we'll have sex now, saving the argument time. Meaning that I'll still be able to feed you and get you to work on time."

"Uh ... I honestly don't know what to say to that."

He's grinning. "*Yes* is the only word you have to say."

I can't stop staring at his handsome face. "You are like no one I have ever known in my life before."

"Good." He smiles. "I'm glad to be your first." He kisses me again. "Now, say, *Yes, Jack, I want to date you.*"

I don't respond even though I might want to.

It's not the right thing to do.

I'm not meant to be happy in this way. I'm not meant to get close to anyone.

But he's also right. This thing between us is inevitable.

Would it be so wrong for me to keep seeing Jack? See where this thing between us goes?

It might lead nowhere. It could all fall apart. I might actually realize in a week that I don't like him.

I mean, I don't see that happening, but you never know.

And … Jack might think the same of me.

He might get bored of my weird ways. Having to have sex with me wearing a tank top all the time. He might think, *Screw this*, and call things off.

I ignore the knot of pain I feel in my chest at the thought of it.

But … in the meantime, I can have some time with him now. Enjoy it before he leaves me. Which he inevitably will.

"Audrey …" Jack murmurs, kissing my jaw.

"Jack …"

"Say, *Yes, Jack, we're dating.*" Another kiss to the corner of my mouth.

His lips hover a breath away. His eyes staring into mine. The smile in them making my heart beat faster.

I let out a sigh. "Okay," I whisper.

"Okay what?"

"Okay, we're dating."

His face expands into a smile right before he kisses me.

"You've made a good choice," he murmurs.

"I hope I don't regret it," I tease.

He eases me onto my back and climbs on top of me, nestling his hips between mine. I feel his cock, already hard, pressing up against my clit, making it throb.

He smiles up at me. "I'll make sure you don't."

After a hard and fast—well, fast for Jack—sex session, we decide to take turns, having a shower.

I go in first. Part of me feels wistful that we can't shower together. But I can't let him see my scars. It's just the way it is, and there is no point in having a pity party over it.

When I get out of the shower, Jack isn't in the bedroom, so I quickly dry off, putting on my bra and pulling on a tank top.

I call out to Jack that I'm finished in the shower, and he replies that he'll be there soon.

It doesn't take me long to finish getting ready. I didn't wash my hair because I'd already washed it last night. So, I brush it out and then plait it, bringing it over my shoulder, checking it in the mirror as I do it. I apply moisturizer to my face. My skin does not like this cold weather, and it's also a little sore from Jack's stubble, as are my lips, so I apply some lip balm to them. Well, actually, a lot of my body is sore. Muscles were used last night that I hadn't even known that I had, and between my legs is a constant reminder that Jack was there.

I know that, all day at the library, I'll be thinking about every moment of last night with him.

Good thing I'm not a guy; otherwise, I would be hiding a stiffy all day long.

That thought makes me chuckle.

Jack walks into the bedroom at that moment. "What's got you laughing?" He drops what looks like clothes on my bed and comes up behind me. Wrapping his arms around me, he presses a kiss to the side of my neck.

"Just thinking that I'm glad I am not a guy."

His eyes meet mine in the mirror, and a smile lifts his lips. "Got to say, I'm glad that you're not a guy too." He kisses my neck again and then releases me. "I made coffee," he tells me. "I wasn't sure what you liked to eat, so I made eggs with some bacon and pancakes."

"I have bacon? And pancake mix?"

"Nope." He grins before disappearing into the bathroom. "But I did. I ran over to my apartment and grabbed the stuff. Feel free to start without me. I'll be quick in the shower."

I walk out of my bedroom into the living room to see breakfast laid out over the countertop, waiting for me.

I can't remember the last time that a guy I slept with made breakfast for me ... which is probably because it was never.

The last time I actually had breakfast made for me was when my adoptive mom was still alive. Sadness pierces my chest at the thought. She always loved to make breakfast in the morning, and Dad and I enjoyed eating what she'd made. Cole, not so much. He's never been a morning person. More of an elusive night owl.

I walk over to the counter, seeing Eleven in the kitchen, eating some kitty food out of a little bowl that Jack must have brought over from his place.

"Morning, cutie." I bend down to pet her, stroking her back, but she's too busy eating to care about me.

I seat myself on one of the two stools I have at my counter. Even though the food looks and smells delicious, I decide to wait for Jack.

I want to eat this breakfast with him.

While I wait, I pour out the coffee into two mugs that Jack put out for us.

I add creamer and sugar to mine and take a sip.

He makes damn good coffee.

I could keep him just for that fact alone.

My eyes drift over to the section of the kitchen counter where Jack fucked me last night.

My whole body heats from just the memory alone.

Sex with Jack is everything I thought it would be and more.

But now that the night is over with, I'm not really sure where we go from here.

I know I shouldn't continue seeing Jack.

But I have proven that when it comes to him, I have zero self-control.

Jack appears from my bedroom, freshly showered. His hair is still damp, and he's wearing a clean T-shirt and jeans. Those must be the clothes he put on my bed. He must have brought them back from his apartment when he went over there.

His feet are bare. I can't help but look at them as he walks over to me.

He has nice feet for a man.

And there is nothing sexier than a man in jeans and bare feet.

He drags out the stool from next to me and sits on it.

Then, he cups the back of my neck and pulls me in for a kiss.

He softly brushes his lips over mine. There is none of the roughness from last night. Just the tender sweep of his lips over mine and the gentle sweep of his tongue in my mouth.

"Needed that," he tells me, pulling back to look in my eyes.

"What?"

"To kiss you."

"You kissed me a few minutes ago." I smile.

"Pretty girl, I could kiss you every second of the day, and it still wouldn't be enough."

Warmth collects in my chest. I'm pretty sure I've got a goofy smile on my face and cartoon hearts in my eyes right now.

Trying to regain some control of myself, I pull back and clear my throat. "I poured you a coffee," I tell him.

"Thank you." He picks it up, and without adding anything to it, he takes a sip.

"Thank you for the food," I tell him. "It smells amazing."

"Let's hope it tastes as good as it smells." He grins.

We eat together, chatting about small stuff.

Jack tells me that his deadline for submission to his publisher is looming close, so he needs to really get moving with his book. He's a little behind.

I ask him about the book, and he tells me about the storyline.

DEAD PRETTY

It's about a man who returns home after his father is found murdered. He and his father didn't get along. His father was physically abusive to him throughout his whole childhood. He left there as soon as he could. While the main character is back in his childhood town, arranging details for his father's funeral, the fingers of accusation start to point his way even though he wasn't even in the state at the time. But evidence starts cropping up, making it seem as though he were there, to the point that he starts to doubt his own sanity and wonders if he was actually there and if he did murder his father.

Even though I have zero interest in fictional crime stories, I do have to admit that the plot sounds brilliant.

I like seeing how animated he becomes when talking about his work. How his eyes seem to brighten even more when he shares his ideas for the story.

I ask how he comes up with the concepts for his books. The mind of a writer has always fascinated me. How they come up with a story. How it forms in their minds.

They build these whole worlds that readers can get lost in. It's incredible.

Jack shrugs and tells me that it just comes naturally to him. Something that he has always been able to do.

An idea will appear, and then it will just grow quickly until it becomes the whole story.

"Do the characters talk to you? Like, you actually hear them in your head?" I ask, dying to know the answer.

He smiles, his lips lifting at one corner. "If I said yes, would you think I was crazy?"

"No." I shake my head. "I've heard before that many writers hear their characters, almost as if they were real people to them."

He chuckles. "My friend …" His eyes move away, looking down at the counter. "The one I mentioned last night."

Something uncomfortable lodges in my chest, and my stomach tightens into a thousand knots. "The one who lives in Australia?"

The same friend who I'm fairly sure is an ex-girlfriend. The person who sent his manuscript off to a publisher. The reason he got his first book deal.

The ex-girlfriend that I think he still has feelings for.

"Yeah. Well, he used to say that there was a fine line between being a writer and having schizophrenia."

"Should I be worried?" I laugh, lifting my brows.

Jack widens his eyes, giving me a crazy look. "Maybe …" He grins.

Sniggering, I get up from my stool and start helping him clean up.

"Leave the plates in the sink," I tell Jack, glancing at the clock. "I really should set off for work. I'll wash them when I get home tonight."

"You sure?"

"I'm sure. Just let me get my things together, and then we can go."

Five minutes later, Jack and I exit my apartment. I've got the helmet he bought me in my hand. He stops by his apartment to put Eleven back in there. He puts down fresh food and water for her and grabs his laptop. Then, we head out.

And Jack holds my hand the whole time.

I can't even explain the way it makes me feel. But it is definitely something that resembles happiness.

We exit the building into the cold air. At least it's not snowing at the moment.

We make our way over to his bike. Jack gets his helmet out of the bag on his bike while I put mine on. I have finally figured out how to fasten it. Though I do miss Jack doing it for me and having him close.

But then I get to have him as close as I want, as often as I want.

That thought makes me smile.

I get on the bike behind Jack. Snuggling in close, I wrap my arms around his waist.

The journey to my work takes all of five minutes. Jack parks the bike. He leaves me at the library doors with a kiss and a promise to see me soon. He's coming in the library to write today, but it doesn't open for the public for another twenty minutes. So, he goes to grab some coffee from the coffee shop.

I head inside the library, thinking about the first time I saw Jack in here. I can't believe it was only a few weeks ago.

A lot has changed in that short period of time.

But I know better than anyone how things can change in the blink of an eye.

Nope. Not going anywhere near those bad thoughts today.

Today is a good day, and nothing is going to spoil it. Especially not thoughts of my past.

TWENTY-TWO

"You look happy today," Margaret comments as I stand in the doorway to her office.

"What?"

"Happy," she repeats. "I said, you look happy."

"Oh."

A normal response would be, *Don't I always look happy?* But I'm not even going to waste my breath saying something that would be a lie because I don't usually look happy.

Happy hasn't been my thing for a long time.

But apparently, I am today.

And I know exactly why.

Jack.

I'm just still not sure if it's a good idea or right and fair for me to be feeling even a scrap of happiness when others can't because of me.

"Well, it's nice to see," she adds when I don't respond further.

"I just came to check on what you need me to do today."

"If you could work on the desk again, that would be a big help."

I don't relish the thought of being on reception and checkout, but I also don't hate the idea as much as I once used to.

Standing at that desk means I will have full view of the library. Where Jack will be sitting.

"No problem. Have you heard anything about Mike?" I ask her.

Her face drops, and I immediately feel bad for bringing it up.

"No," she says quietly.

"Sorry, I didn't mean to upset you," I'm quick to say.

She gives me an unhappy smile. "You didn't. It's just the situation as a whole is sad."

I nod my agreement. "I'm sure everything will be fine," I tell her, not knowing if it will be and knowing what things can be like when they're not. "They will find Mike, and everything will get cleared up. Try not to worry."

"Yes, I'm sure you're right." She gives me another forced smile.

"Well … I'll head over to the main desk," I tell her.

"Would you mind opening up the doors for me?" she asks before I leave.

"Of course."

"Let me just get you the keys."

I wait while she rummages around in her bag before she finds them and holds them out for me to take.

"Don't worry about bringing them back, just leave them in the drawer under the counter. I'll get them later."

"Will do." I take the keys from her outstretched hand and then make my way through the library to open up.

I feel bad for bringing Margaret down just then. But it's not long before my thoughts are back to Jack, and I'm smiling again.

But my happy bubble doesn't last for long when Detectives Sparks and Peters walk through the doors of the library only minutes after I unlocked them.

The computer we use to check out books hasn't even had a chance to fire up when they come strolling in.

I put the keys in the drawer, like Margaret asked me to, and wait for the detectives to approach.

I start to feel a nervous, jittery sensation in my body. Worrying that they know who I really am. What my past is.

"Good morning," I say to them when they reach the desk.

The library is empty, except for me and the detectives.

Our other staff member, Derek, is in the upstairs stacks, putting yesterday's returned books away.

"Audrey Hayes," Detective Sparks says my name. There is an edge to his tone that I don't like. "We're here to speak with your boss. Is she here?"

"I'm here," Margaret says, coming up behind me. "Do you have news of Mike?" she asks them.

"Can we talk somewhere private?" Detective Peters says.

"We can talk here. As you can see, there is only us here."

Detective Sparks's eyes flicker to me.

"I can leave you alone." I go to move, but Margaret stops me with a hand on my arm.

"Stay. Please, Detectives, can you tell us what is going on?"

"We recovered a male body late last night, which we identified through dental records as Michael King."

Margaret gasps next to me, covering her mouth with her hand. I'm just standing here, not knowing how to react. What to do.

Hearing about death is not new to me.

"Ho-how did he die?" Margaret asks.

"We can't determine cause of death until the autopsy is done. I hate to ask … but we have been unable to locate a next of kin. Do you know anything of Michael's family?"

Margaret shakes her head. "He didn't have one. He came from foster care. His parents died when he was young. No other family. I think he was close to one of his foster parents. I'm not sure of her name though …" She's shaking her head, clearly distressed.

"Don't worry. We can locate his details through the local foster agencies now that we know that is where we need to be looking," Detective Peters says.

I can feel eyes watching me. Detective Sparks is just staring at me.

It's unnerving as hell.

I look away, turning to Margaret, giving him the side of my head.

Her eyes are wet with tears. She gets a tissue from her pocket, dabbing at her eyes.

"I just can't believe it," Margaret says.

I put my arm around her. It seems like the right thing to do. "I know; it's awful," I say to her.

"Do you know if there is any connection between whoever killed Mike and the person who killed Sarah?" Margaret says.

"We're not at liberty to say," Detective Peters says. "We are sorry to be the ones to deliver this news and also for your loss. We'll be on our way now. But if you think of anything that could be important—"

"I'll call you," Margaret assures the detective.

"And you too," I hear Detective Sparks say, and I turn my eyes to meet his. "The same applies to you, Miss Hayes. If you think of anything that could help us in relation to this case or the death of Sarah Greenwood, then make sure you call us."

I hold his eyes and nod. "Of course."

I watch the detectives leave, a queasy feeling in my stomach.

I hear Margaret sniffling, pulling my attention back to her.

"I just can't believe he's gone," she says. "I know we weren't super close, but it's still so hard to hear."

"I know," I say, trying to comfort her. "Why don't you take the rest of the day off and go home? I'll hold down the fort here."

Her gaze meets with mine. I feel a pang of sympathy at the tears in her eyes. She is such a kind person.

"Yes, I might do that. Thank you, Audrey." She pats my arm with her hand. "You still have the keys to lock up later?"

"They're in the drawer," I tell her. "I can bring them by your house on my way home—"

"Not necessary." She waves me off. "I have a spare set at home. Take the keys home with you and then just bring them back in the morning."

"Okay," I respond.

She gives me another sad smile. "Well, I'll just grab my purse, and then I'll be off."

"Don't worry about anything here. I'll be fine."

Another smile, this one a little brighter. "I know. Thanks again, Audrey."

Jack walks into the library fifteen minutes later. His laptop bag over his shoulder, two coffees in his hand.

His eyes seek me out, and a big smile lights up his face.

I love that I bring that smile to his lips.

He walks over to the reception desk.

"Hey." He sets one of the coffees down on the counter for me. "I brought you a coffee."

"I need it. Thanks."

"Rough day already?" he teases. "It's only been forty minutes."

A lot can happen in forty minutes.

"The police were here a bit ago. Mike ... they found his body. He's dead."

"Jesus," Jack breathes. "Did they say what happened to him?"

I shake my head. "No. They said they can't give out details regarding an open investigation. They only came here to inform Margaret and to ask if she knew of his next of kin."

"Poor guy."

"Yeah. It's awful. Margaret was terribly upset. I said I would stay late and close up the library for her, so she could go home."

"You're a good person." He's smiling at me in that way he does. Like he sees something in me. Something good.

The only problem is, if he keeps looking at me like that, making me feel this way, then I might just start to believe it for myself. And that would be a problem.

"It's not a big deal." I brush his words off. "Still doing my same job. The only difference is, I'll be locking up the place."

"So, that means you have the keys to the library." There's a suggestive tone to his voice. His brow lifts. Eyes glinting with that sex look of his that makes my stomach tighten and the spot between my legs start to tingle.

"It does."

He leans closer. His mouth only a few inches from mine. "I could hang around today. Spend the day writing. Help you lock up later …" His smile is all foxlike. "I mean, I wouldn't want you here, all alone, in this big, old library. Doesn't seem safe."

My stomach muscles all clench, creating a delicious feeling between my legs. "No"—I shake my head—"it doesn't."

The smile that we share in this moment is something that is ours only.

I don't need the words to know that Jack wants us to do it … well, that he wants to do me … in here after I close the library doors for the day.

And I am fully on board with that.

Like I would ever say no to having sex with Jack anywhere.

And doing it here, when no one else is around, just him and me in this big, old library, it seems incredibly hot.

As does the anticipation. Knowing that I will have to wait all day to feel him. Kiss him. Take him inside me. All the while watching him from across the room while he works on his book.

Can anyone say sexy as hell?

Sweet Lord, I am a lucky girl.

I know I've done nothing to deserve this. But I'm holding on to it while I can.

I know that's selfish, but it is hard to be anything else around Jack. I want him so much.

Jack taps his fingers on the counter, that sensual smile lingering. "Enjoy your coffee, pretty girl. I'm going to get some writing done. See you later." He winks, and on anyone else, it would look stupid. But on him, it looks damn good.

Then, he walks away toward the area where the desks are, and I stare at his ass the whole time.

TWENTY-THREE

Today has been actual torture.

I thought the anticipation of waiting for sex with Jack would be a good thing. And it is. Kind of.

But with the object of my desire sitting across the room all day, looking his usual gorgeous self, while I watch him write—with the furrow on his brow when he's thinking, the stroke of his pen against his notebook when he's making notes, the sight of his fingers … fingers that I am well acquainted with and wholly aware of their capabilities and the levels of desire they can bring to me—well, I've just been getting more and more turned on as the day has gone on.

I'm actually sweating. All day, I have been distracted by thoughts of Jack and sex. My thighs have been pressed together more than once today in an attempt to ease the ache. News flash: it doesn't work. My body is overstimulated. Every time my nipples brush against the lace of my bra, it's actual agony.

And trust me, when you're waiting for something, the clock has a tendency to slow down to a snail's pace, and the clock on the wall here has been annoyingly creeping through the minutes.

It has been a long-ass day.

Half a dozen times, I've been tempted to just drag Jack to the women's restroom with me, so he could screw me right there and then.

But I honestly haven't had a spare minute to even take him to the restroom with me even if I dared to do it. The worry of getting caught and letting Margaret down has been playing with my conscience. Even though the horny devil on my shoulder has definitely been pushing for a restroom quickie.

With Margaret not being here, I have been handling everything that she does on a daily basis as well as doing my own duties.

We're a staff member down with Mike ... well, with him gone.

It has been a lot to take on.

I didn't realize the half of what managing a library consists of.

It makes me glad that I'm only a librarian and not the manager of one.

Running a library is not on my list of things to do ever again.

I breathe a sigh of relief when it's time to finally shut the doors and lock them up for the night.

Jack is working on his laptop when I walk over to lock the doors after the last person leaves.

When I turn back around, I see Jack is away from the desk now. He's standing by the window, staring out of it. The windows down here are privacy glass. You can see out, but no one can see in.

It's still light outside. The evening only early. Snow is falling again.

I stare at his profile for a moment, taking in the strong line of his shoulders. How his jeans mold to his tight ass. The way his hair curls at the nape of his neck. Remembering how it felt to run my fingers over that very spot.

He turns, looking over his shoulder, catching me staring.

I have two choices. Look away and pretend I wasn't watching. Or smile and admit defeat.

I go for the latter. At this point, pretending anything with Jack seems fruitless.

He grins in return.

I wander over to where he's standing, taking the spot beside him.

"What are you thinking about?" I ask him softly. Even though it's only the two of us right now, it still feels odd to speak in a louder voice in here.

Our eyes meet in the reflection in the glass.

His lips lift at one side. "You."

Goose bumps break out over my skin at his word. Desire coiling low in my stomach.

"Awfully pensive look on your face to be thinking about me," I tease.

His eyes move from our mirrored connection to look directly into mine. "I'm never pensive when I think about you, Audrey. Only horny."

That makes me laugh. "You're incorrigible."

"You've made me this way with your sexiness."

I'm pretty sure my eyeroll can be heard across the room. "Sure I have."

"You have."

He turns his body toward mine. Taking my hand, he tugs me into his chest. "I have never been this hot for anyone before."

It's on the tip of my tongue to ask him about his ex-girlfriends. See if he'll open up to me about the one in Australia.

But I chicken out. Because if I ask Jack questions, then he will be at liberty to ask me. And I don't want to answer anything about my past.

"So, you have a thing for library sex, huh?" I grin up at him.

He smirks. "I'm a writer. Sex among the greats is like a wet dream for me."

I laugh. "Ever done it in a library before?" I ask. It's a stupid question to ask because I've literally just broken my own *don't ask questions* rule. God, I'm dumb.

I guess my need to know if I'll be the first to have sex with him in a library or if I'm just one of many library fucks that he's partaken in overruled any good sense I had.

Jack's fingers move to the band holding my hair in a braid. He pulls it out, letting my hair fall down my back and around my shoulders. He fingers a lock of it. "First time. You?"

I won't even try to deny how much it thrills me, knowing this is a first for him too.

"Never."

"Good. Now, let's lose our library virginities." His lips crash down onto mine.

His tongue insanely seeks entry. I part my lips on a breath, letting our tongues tangle together.

He tastes like the sweet remnants of coffee and the gum he's been chewing on and off throughout the day.

His fingers thread through my hair. My hands grip his waist as we devour one another's mouths.

I'm moving backward.

Jack is guiding me toward the table he has spent the day writing at.

But I have other ideas.

Pressing my hand to his chest, I break the kiss.

I take a step back away from him. "Stay," is my softly commanded order.

My trembling fingers go to the buttons on my shirt. I slowly start to unbutton it.

Jack watches me with dark, hooded eyes.

My eyes skim down his body. His erection is visible and straining against his jeans.

It gives me a boost of confidence that any girl needs in order to do a striptease in front of a man. Her man.

Because that is what Jack is.

My man ... the guy I'm dating ... sleeping with ... although we won't be doing any sleeping anytime soon.

I reach the last button, the fabric parting, and slip the shirt off my shoulders, letting it fall to the floor, leaving me in my tank and bra.

Kicking a shoe off, I take another step backward.

Jack stays standing where he is, watching my every move. I see his hands fisting at his sides, like it is taking everything in him not to come to me.

I'm moving, shedding clothes as I go until I reach my destination. The first row of bookshelves.

When my back presses up against the books, I'm left in only my panties and tank top.

Jack is still fully clothed.

I hook my fingers into the band of my panties and shimmy them down my hips until they hit the floor.

I wish I could remove my top, finish the whole striptease for him, but I can't. I'm not ready. I might not ever be ready.

Biting my lip, I look up at Jack through my lashes.

He looks like he is physically restraining himself to stay where he is.

Grinning, I lift my index finger and gesture for him to come to me.

Only I don't expect him to move so fast.

He is on me in seconds.

His mouth back on mine.

He nips my bottom lip with his teeth. "I've waited for you all fucking day, Audrey. No more waiting. I'm fucking you now." His words are sexy, hot, and everything in between, and they turn me on so much.

"Yes," I gasp. The word echoes around the large room.

Jack's mouth moves down my neck, kissing and biting.

My hands race to unfasten his jeans.

His go between my legs. He pushes a finger inside me.

"God, Jack," I moan, my head thudding back against the books.

He growls this sexy-as-hell sound.

His T-shirt comes off.

I somehow manage to finish getting his jeans undone and push them down over his ass, taking his boxers with them. Neither of us bothers to remove them fully.

He grabs a condom from the front pocket of his jeans, and he rolls it on with deft hands.

How he is this steady right now, I will never know.

I'm a shaking, writhing mess.

Jack and I have never had sex this quickly before. He usually likes to have foreplay. Lots of it. But then we have never had sex anywhere but in my apartment.

Right now, he seems desperate to be inside me, and I am all for it.

His hand yanks down the top of my tank, and his mouth covers my nipple, sucking and biting.

My hands go instantly to his head, gripping the soft strands of his hair.

His lips make a path up my chest, back to my mouth, kissing me once.

Then, he rests his forehead to mine. Our noses aligned.

My chest is heaving. My breaths unsteady. About as unsteady as my trembling body. I'm shaking with desire and need.

My eyes blink open and stare into Jack's.

And it's in that moment, when our eyes lock, that the connection between us explodes into something otherworldly. Wild and untamed. Like nothing I have known before.

His hand grips my thigh. He lifts it around his hip.

Then, he thrusts up inside me, his eyes not leaving mine.

I expect him to fuck me, but he doesn't.

He kisses me. Gently. Almost reverently. A total contrast to the way his hard cock is inside me, ready to fuck me fast and hard against this bookcase.

"I'm crazy about you, Audrey." His words are a loud whisper in the silence of this large room.

My heart fills to the point of bursting.

"I'm crazy about you too," I tell him.

"Just … no matter what happens between you and me … know that I will always want you. Always."

My heart thuds hard against my rib cage.

He sounds so serious. It worries me but also makes me feel the need to soothe him.

I cup his face in my hands. "Only good things happen between us, Jack," I tell him right before I press my mouth to his, kissing him.

I coax his lips to part with mine.

It doesn't take long before he's back with me and controlling our kiss. His mouth devouring mine, tongue plundering. Holding me exactly where he wants me.

The desire that Jack has for me, it's as addictive as he tastes.

"Fuck me, Jack," I whisper against his mouth.

And he does. He fucks me right there against the bookcase. Arms above my head, my wrists bound by his hand, one leg hooked around his hip, his cock deep inside me.

And my heart in his hands.

TWENTY-FOUR

I wake with a start. My eyes flash open. I bolt upright. Heart thumping in my chest.

There's someone in the room. A shadow in the corner.

Parting my lips to scream, I blink.

And it's gone.

No one is there.

My eyes scan around the room.

I press my hand to my chest, my heart beating wildly.

It must have been the remnants of a dream. A nightmare.

It's not the first time this has happened to me. Thinking there's someone there. Seeing the shadow of a person, haunting me.

I guess it's not surprising after everything I've been through.

My eyes move to Jack lying beside me. Asleep on his stomach. Arms stretched up above his head. His face turned toward me.

He looks beautiful. The shadows lining his face. The glow of the light from the hall framing it.

I'm tempted to touch him. But I don't want to wake him. He looks so peaceful.

Checking the time on my cell, I see that it's only ten thirty.

We came to bed early. We started watching a movie on Netflix in bed, using Jack's laptop, but got distracted by each other.

We must have fallen asleep after screwing each other senseless.

Getting off the bed, I search for my discarded pajama shorts on the floor.

Locating them, I pull them on. Taking my phone with me, I quietly make my way into the living room, heading for the kitchen to get a drink of water.

Eleven is asleep on the sofa. She lifts her head as I pass and then lays it straight back down.

She spends a lot of time over here now. As does Jack.

I like them both here.

I know I don't deserve the happiness that I have right now, but I'm reluctant to let it go.

The thought of losing Jack fills me with a hollowness that I can't even contemplate.

I get a glass from the cupboard and pour myself a water from the purifier in the fridge, bringing it over to the sofa with me. I take a seat next to Eleven, tucking my legs underneath me. I stroke her soft fur.

She starts to purr, snuggling closer to me.

It makes me smile.

Tapping my screen, bringing it to life, I see that I have some notifications. They're from local news sites.

With Detectives Sparks and Peters not willing to tell us anything about Mike's death, the only resource left to me is the press.

In the days following the discovery of Mike's body, I have learned that he was found in the closet of Sarah's apartment, his body hidden behind some luggage stored in there. It had been missed in the first search of Sarah's apartment when her body was first discovered. A screwup on the part of the police department.

They initially found two blood types at the crime scene. Knowing one was Mike's, they first thought he was the killer and that he'd most likely cut himself in the attack on Sarah.

But he hadn't.

Mike had been stabbed to death. Thirty stab wounds found on his stomach, chest, and hands. The press said they were defensive wounds on his hands. They said the knife pierced his heart, which was the killing blow.

A violent murder.

In contrast, Sarah had been tortured.

Knife wounds were found all over her body.

She had been cut close to a hundred times.

Then, finally, her throat was slit.

She hadn't been stabbed like Mike.

The news said it was likely that Mike had interrupted the killer, and that was why his wounds were in such stark contrast to Sarah's.

Mike wasn't her killer.

And she was murdered in a very similar way to the other recent murders.

Am I afraid?

Yes.

All of the murders are comparable to the murders that Tobias committed in Chicago.

I'm trying not to freak out. Link them together. Let my mind believe that there is a copycat here. But it's really hard not to think that way.

The only thing keeping me sane at the moment is Jack.

Not that he knows the depths of my thoughts. He knows I have an interest in what happened to Mike and Sarah because I worked with Mike. But Jack doesn't know my thoughts on the other murders.

Because if he did, then I would have to tell him about my past.

And that is the last thing I want.

My cell vibrates in my hand, startling me.

A look at the screen tells me it's Cole. It's not unusual for him to call me late. He's a night owl.

It's been a little over a week since I last spoke to him now that I think about it.

He's not going to be happy with me. I'm supposed to call once a week.

It's just that I have been distracted by the man currently sleeping in my bed.

Not that I'll be sharing that nugget of information with Cole.

He won't be keen on me dating someone that he hasn't had the opportunity to meet and vet.

Having an overprotective brother can be a pain at times. But I understand why he is the way he is.

Smiling, I apprehensively answer the call, putting the phone to my ear.

"Hey," I say softly.

"So, you are alive then?" He sounds like he's teasing, but he knows better than to say things like that to me, meaning he's pissed but disguising it.

"I'm sorry. I should have called."

"Yes, you should have. What's been keeping you so busy?"

I can't tell him that one of my coworkers was murdered alongside his girlfriend. Cole would lose his mind and order me home straightaway.

Not that I would go.

I can't leave Jack.

I know that deep inside my heart. The heart that Jack has reawakened within me.

But I also don't want to upset my brother. So, the best thing to do is to tell him nothing.

"Work. One of the guys who worked there … he quit. So, we're down an employee. And my boss has been out sick for a few days as well, so I've been running the place in her absence. Early mornings, late evenings."

"You shouldn't let them overwork you, Audrey."

"I'm not. I'm just helping out. My boss is a nice lady. She would never take advantage."

The line goes silent. I hate when Cole goes quiet on me.

"I made a new friend," I tell him.

"Oh?" I can hear the interest in his voice. "And what is this new friend called?"

"Gary."

Another pause. I'm fighting a smile. Not that he can see it right now.

But somehow, my brother has the ability to see and know most things about me.

"A man?"

"Uh-huh." I can no longer fight the grin, and it spreads over my whole face.

"Are you dating him?"

"You could say that."

Jack and I have been walking Gary and Pork Chop every lunchtime this week. I have been busy with work, but I have made time to walk those guys at lunch. I love walking them with Jack. It makes me happy.

Jack makes me happy.

"I spend my lunch hour with him."

"Audrey—"

"He's about four years old," I cut him off, sniggering quietly to myself. "Has gray-and-white fur …"

"A fucking dog." Cole laughs, and the sound puts joy into my heart.

I don't hear Cole laugh much anymore.

"Yes. He's a rescue dog. He lives at the rescue center near the library. I've started walking him on my lunch hour. He's so sweet. You would love him."

"If you let me come to you, then I would be able to meet him."

I sigh. "Cole …"

"I know; I know. I'll stop talking."

"No, don't ever stop talking to me. *Please.*" I can feel this odd sense of panic quickly rising up in my chest. I press the heel of my hand to my sternum, trying to stem the fear.

"That's not what I meant, Audrey, and you know that. I will never leave you. *Never.*"

I exhale. "I know." The panic starts to abate in my chest at the forcefulness of his words.

Of course Cole would never leave me. What was I thinking?

But I did leave him. He has always been there for me, and I just walked away from him.

I'm a terrible person and sister.

I'm selfish.

Even more so because I don't know when I'm going back home. Or if I ever will.

"You should get yourself to bed," Cole says softly in my ear. "You need your sleep."

"Yeah. You're right." I yawn.

He knows me so well.

There's another pause and then, "I love you, Audrey."

I smile. There's a tinge of sadness that I hope he doesn't hear when I say, "I love you too, Cole."

I hang up the call. Holding the phone in my hand, I stare down at the dark screen.

"Who were you on the phone with?"

My head whips up to see a shirtless Jack standing in the doorway. He's wearing just his sleep pants. His hair is all mussed up. He looks adorable.

"My brother," I answer without thinking, caught off guard by the sight of him.

I lower my cell phone to the sofa, putting it on the arm.

Jack comes over and sits by me. Eleven is now squished between us. She doesn't seem pleased by this at all and jumps down from the sofa, wandering into the direction of my bedroom.

"You have a brother?" Jack says quietly beside me.

I bring my eyes to him and nod.

There's a flash of something in his eyes that I can't quite decipher and a little line between his brows.

I know that happens when he's thinking intently about something. Which is why I ask, "You're frowning. Why?"

"I'm not."

I press my finger against the little crease, rubbing it out.

"That's just called old age."

I laugh. "You are older than me, so it makes sense you'd wrinkle first."

He rests his head back against the sofa, eyes still on me. "Does it bother you that I'm older?"

I shake my head. "Does it bother you?"

"No." He's still watching me.

I know there's more he wants to say, and the anticipation jangles my nerves.

"So, you have a brother …"

And there it is.

Jack lets the words hang in the air.

"Yes."

"Does he live close by?"

"No."

He nods in response to my answer. "Any other siblings?"

"No. Why all the questions?" My voice is a little sharper than I intended. But I don't want to have this conversation about my brother. Because it will lead to my adoptive parents and their deaths, possibly even my biological parents, and I really don't want to talk about any of them right now. I don't want to talk with Jack about my past, period.

"Just wondering if I need to look out for more than one brother who will want to kick my ass for screwing his sister." His eyes are smiling, but the lines around his mouth are tight.

I've upset him with my harsh tone. I hate that I have.

I don't like that I'm so messed up. I wish I were different for him.

Jack and I are in this pseudo relationship, where neither of us really knows the other.

All I know about Jack is that he was in the military, he's an author, and he fucks like a god.

And all he knows about me is that I have a brother.

We know so very little about each other.

How can we have a real relationship when we don't know anything about each other?

And is a real relationship what I want with Jack?

I'm happy with the way things are right now.

"Sorry," I say, laying my head back on the sofa, looking at him in the eyes.

"What for?"

"Because …" I let the word drift off because, really, what do I say? *Sorry that I'm shut up like a locked box? That I'm a bitch? That I'm a crap girlfriend?* Take your pick.

He reaches a hand over and brushes my hair behind my ear. "You don't have anything to be sorry for, Audrey." He smiles at me.

I know he's letting me off, and I love him for it.

And I do.

Love him.

Completely and madly.

I don't need to know this man's past to love him. Only the him in the now.

And maybe he doesn't need to know mine to care for me.

This here is who we are. Together. And that is all that matters.

"Well, except for …"

I tense at his words.

"The fact that you're sitting all the way over there."

I immediately relax. "I'm sitting right next to you."

"Like I said … too far." He pats his lap with his hand.

Fighting a smile, I get up and straddle his lap, my legs going on either side of his. "Happy?" I ask him.

He tips his head back, staring up at me. "Hang on."

His hands grab hold of both my ass cheeks, and he shifts me forward, putting me right against his hardening dick. My hands land on his chest as that zip of energy that I always feel with him makes its way through my body.

"Now, I am." His eyes grin up at me.

"Are you ever not horny?" I can hear how breathless I already sound.

How can I go from worried to horny in a few moments?
Him.

Jack is the reason.

"Around you?" He smirks. "Nope."

I slide my hands up his chest, putting my arms around the back of his neck, bringing our faces close together.

I stare into his eyes, wanting to tell him everything that I feel for him.

The one thing I hadn't felt until he walked into my life.

Happy.

Such a singular word. A small word. But it means so much to me.

He means so much to me.

"You make me happy," I tell him, hoping that I make the importance of these words known.

He likes that. I see the way his face changes into a smile.

"You make me happy too. And ... you'll make me even happier right now if you slip out of those sleep shorts"—he tugs on the fabric of them—"and then climb back up here on my lap and sit yourself down on my dick."

He winks, and I laugh.

I'm not laughing a moment later when he puts his mouth on mine and kisses me.

The feel of his lips on mine ... it is electric. Every molecule of my being pays attention when Jack touches me.

When he's with me like this, I feel like there is no more me. Just us. I drown in him, and I like it more than I can say.

I slide my hands up into his hair. Fingers sifting through the silky, wavy strands.

Something feels different about this moment. I don't have the words to explain it.

Just ... his kiss is softer, gentler. Searching.

I'm not wholly sure what it is he's seeking from within me, but I am here for it.

I'm here for him. With him.

There is nowhere else I would ever want to be.

He exhales, and it tickles my lips.

Then, the kiss turns deep. Endless.

Each sweep of his mouth over mine runs together, creating a never-ending kiss.

I squirm restlessly in his lap, needing more contact.

He makes no move to give it to me.

His hands slide up my back, into my hair, fingers tangling into the strands, while his tongue continues stroking mine.

Then, his fingers move to my neck, tracing a line down to my shoulders.

I want his hands on my breasts. But they just stay there, teasing circles on the skin of my shoulders.

I don't know where Jack is going to take this moment. But I'm more than ready and willing to go wherever he wants.

A finger slides under the strap of my tank and moves lower.

Yes.

But instead of dragging the cup down to free my breast, like he normally would, his finger just trails a path over the swell of my breast.

It's the sweetest form of torture.

His mouth leaves mine and kisses a path across my jaw to my ear. Teeth grazing the lobe, his breath hot and flirting with my skin, he whispers, "I'm crazy about you, Audrey."

His words … his touch … make me shiver.

His mouth moves down my neck. I tip my head back, giving him access.

The hint of tongue on my skin, and I'm ready to combust.

But still, he hasn't put a hand on my breast or down my pants.

My important bits are screaming for attention.

"Jack," I moan. I shift myself forward, closer to his hard cock, needing to press myself against it.

When I make contact, my eyes close, and I see stars behind my lids.

Jack's mouth finds mine again. He moans as his tongue sweeps inside my mouth.

His hand palms my lower back, and I start to slowly ride him through the thin material of our sleep clothes.

"Audrey," he whispers my name, and it sounds like a prayer.

One I'm more than happy to answer.

"I want to see you."

Does he mean ... he wants to see all of me? Or see me how he usually sees me?

Part of me is afraid to ask.

But a part of me is also tired of hiding who I am.

I want Jack. I want him to know me.

But if I take my shirt off ... if I show him the scars ... will it change the way he looks at me? The way he wants me?

If Jack had scars like I do, would it change the way I wanted him?

No. Of course it wouldn't.

So, why do I think it will change the way he looks at me?

Because I'm afraid.

Fear.

It controls every aspect of my life.

I don't want to be afraid anymore.

Especially not with Jack.

Breaking our kiss, I slide off Jack's lap and stand in front of him.

I don't know where this sudden bout of confidence has come from, but I don't want to lose it.

I hook my fingers into the waistband of my shorts and pull them down.

Jack's eyes are fixed on me. I love the way he looks at me. Like I'm the only thing in the world he sees.

But will he still look at me the same when he sees my scars? Stop. Don't think that way.

Jack is silent. Watching me.

I'm scared. My insides are quaking.

I'm about to reveal the worst thing about me.

I might not be vocalizing it. Telling him my past. What happened to me. Where these scars came from.

But I will be telling him that something happened to me.

I'll be making myself vulnerable to him.

And it's absolutely fucking terrifying.

My hands are shaking as they reach for the hem of my tank top.

I see the change in Jack's expression when he realizes what I'm about to do.

But his expression isn't one of curiosity. It's admiration. Because he knows exactly how hard this is for me.

And that gives me the last boost of confidence I need to lift my top up and over my head, exposing my ugly, physical flaw to him.

My eyes are closed. I'm afraid to open them. Afraid of what I'll see when I look at Jack.

"Audrey." His deep, soft voice reverberates over my skin.

Taking a strengthening breath, I open my eyes.

Jack is standing now.

His eyes on mine.

I'm naked … completely defenseless in front of him.

My heart is beating fast. My body vibrating with nerves.

I feel raw. Like someone took a grater to my insides.

Jack's hand lifts to my face, cupping my cheek.

I stare up into his eyes. Those eyes I just can't seem to ever look away from.

"You are beautiful, Audrey." His voice is raspy. "You are always beautiful."

In this moment, it feels as if a dark cloud lifts off me. A barrier gone between us.

And nothing matters but Jack and me.

Not my past. The scars on my skin.

Nothing.

Just him and me.

I reach up on my toes and press my lips to his.

The kiss turns molten in seconds.

Jack picks me up, and my arms and legs go around his hard body.

He carries me back to bed.

Laying me down, he stays with me. On top of me. Still kissing me.

My hands push down his pajama pants, getting them down his legs. Jack helps get them off, kicking them aside.

Then, there is nothing between us.

No more fabric barriers.

Jack breaks the kiss. Pressing his forehead to mine, he stares into my eyes.

There are no words spoken between us. There doesn't need to be. We're saying everything there is to say with our eyes.

Yes, I want you. I want this.

The first push of Jack inside me feels so different to all the other times yet so incredibly familiar.

When he is fully inside of me, his lips seek mine.

He kisses me gently, sweetly. He's deep inside of me. Unmoving. And I have never felt closer to him than I do right now.

"Beautiful," he whispers, his mouth moving down my neck. "So fucking beautiful, Audrey. I can't get enough of you. Nothing will ever be enough."

His lips find my nipple, and he sucks it into his mouth.

Desire shoots through my core.

"Fuck me, Jack. *Please.*"

His eyes lift to mine.

He slowly pulls out of me and then pushes back inside, equally as leisurely.

It is exquisite torture.

And it feels an awful lot like making love.

Jack's pace stays that way, unhurried. His hands hold mine above my head, his mouth on mine, as he screws me with his cock.

I'm a writhing, needy mess beneath him.

My orgasm comes quickly and without warning, taking me by surprise.

My hands grip his, my cry of pleasure swallowed by his mouth.

Then, Jack's moaning my name against my lips, and I feel him start to come too.

When we're both finished coming down from our highs, Jack kisses me again. A loving kiss.

Still inside me, he lays his head down on the pillow, burying his face in my neck.

DEAD PRETTY

And we fall asleep just like that—with Jack buried deep inside of me in all the ways that matter.

TWENTY-FIVE

I blink.

There was a knock at the door.

God, I totally zoned out then. This is what I get for watching pointless television while Jack is in the shower and I'm waiting for our dinner to be delivered.

I give Eleven's fur a ruffle before I get up from the sofa and go to answer the door.

I pause before opening it. It might not be my apartment, but there is always that wariness inside of me.

Especially with Mike's and Sarah's recent murders and the murders of those other women and no suspect in sight, according to the press.

Does my mind go to Tobias when I think about these recent killings?

Yes.

Am I still worrying about a copycat?

Yes-ish.

Tobias never killed a man when he went on his rampage.

But then maybe that's because he was never interrupted by one, like Sarah's killer was.

Or maybe Tobias has killed a man before, and people just don't know it.

Scrapping those thoughts before I get lost in them, I lift onto my tiptoes and peer through the peephole.

It's a young, dark-haired guy with a pizza box in hand.

I open the door, smiling at him.

"Hey, that'll be fifteen dollars."

He hands me the pizza. Smells yummy. Jack and I went for one of those half-and-half pizzas. He likes olives on his. Gross.

"Just let me get my purse," I tell the delivery guy.

I leave the door ajar. Putting the pizza on the coffee table, I grab my bag from the side of the sofa. I get my wallet out and open it up.

Huh. There's no money in it.

I'm sure there was a twenty in here this morning. Like, ninety percent sure.

That is so weird.

Well, no time to think about it now. I put my purse back in my bag and call out Jack's name.

I hear the water turn off, and then his deep voice says, "Yeah?"

"Pizza's here, and I have no cash."

"My wallet is on the kitchen counter. Should be some money in there."

Thank God. Otherwise, one of us would have been making a quick dash to the nearest ATM.

I find Jack's wallet where he said it would be. Flip it open and see a couple of tens in there.

Perfect.

I pull the cash out. Something drops out from in between them.

It flutters to the floor.

I peer down at it.

It's a small piece of blank paper. About half the size of the bills in my hand.

I bend down and pick it up. I turn it over to see what, if anything, is on the other side.

It's a section from a news article. Like the type people can print out from the computers at the library.

It takes me a moment before it registers in my brain who and what this article is about. And then it does, and my whole body freezes cold.

It's about Tobias Ripley. Before the murders. When he was a senior in high school. Some award he won.

And there's a picture accompanying the article.

I recognize Tobias's mother standing beside him. I know her from his trial.

But it's who is standing on the other side of Tobias with his arm around his shoulders that causes pain to slice across my stomach, where my scars are.

I feel like I'm back there that night.

But instead of it being Tobias who cut me, this time, it's Jack.

And this feels so much worse than any pain Tobias ever inflicted on me.

Because that person smiling in the picture with his arm around Tobias's shoulders is Jack.

My Jack.

TWENTY-SIX

I'm running on autopilot when I pay the pizza guy and close the door.

And I just stand here. Staring at nothing.

Jack knows Tobias.

I let this man inside my body. I cared for him … loved him.

And all that time … he knew … Tobias.

I stare down at the news clipping, still held in my hand.

Bile floods my mouth.

Jack … he …

I … have to understand this. How Jack knows him. And why he's here. With me.

It's obviously no coincidence. Meaning that he came here for me.

Why?

To kill me?

My heart beats staccato against my ribs.

No. Jack could have done that a hundred times over already. That is not the reason he's here. He's here for another reason.

But what?

I hear Jack moving around. His footsteps enter the living room.

"Pizza smells good," he says from behind me. "Audrey? Why are you standing there, staring at the door?"

Slowly, I turn around.

The carefree, slightly confused look on his face morphs into something else. Concern. Worry.

"Audrey, what's wrong?" It's evident in his voice too.

I part my lips, but I can't seem to get any words out. I feel like my tongue is glued to the roof of my mouth.

I look back down at the picture. It's like I'm willing my brain to tell me that I have this wrong.

But I don't.

He knows the man who tormented and tortured me.

"What's that?" he asks.

I lift my eyes to his. He gestures to the paper in my hand.

There is nothing in his expression that gives anything away.

I swallow thickly. "It fell out of your wallet."

He frowns. "It did?"

"How do you know Tobias Ripley, Jack?"

My words seem to slam into the room, taking all the color from Jack's face with them.

"What are you talking about?" I hear the waver in his voice.

I try to control the sudden onslaught of rage that I feel inside of me.

My hand holding the photo trembles. "Tobias Ripley. How do you know him, Jack?"

"I don't know—"

"Don't fucking lie!" I yell. My quick anger breaks into the room, like Jack broke into my life.

I take a step forward and toss the paper with the picture of him and Tobias toward him.

Jack picks it up from the floor.

I step back, closer to the door. Needing a quick exit if this goes south.

Not that I think Jack would ever hurt me.

But then I never suspected that he knew Tobias.

So, there is that.

I watch him studying the picture. He takes a deep breath.

Every movement and sound seems incredibly pronounced in this moment.

His eyes lift back to mine. Still, there is nothing in them to tell me anything. Not a hint of emotion.

Just blank. Empty.

Kind of like both of our souls.

"Where did you get this?"

"Your wallet."

"That's not possible. I never put this—"

"I don't care!" I yell. "What I care about is how you know Tobias Ripley! Why you're in a photograph with him and his mother!"

The silence that ensues is heavy. Like a weighted blanket covering my body. But there is no comfort with this. Just the feeling of entrapment and suffocation.

Jack drags a hand through his hair.

He can't seem to look at me. It's telling because Jack usually can't keep his eyes off me.

"I am going to ask one last time. How. Do. You. Know. Tobias. Ripley?"

Finally, those eyes I believed I loved look into mine. "I know Tobias because he's my … brother."

TWENTY-SEVEN

In my life, I have been hit, tied up, and held against my will. Had my skin cut open with a knife.

And none of those compare to the pain that I'm feeling right now.

Tobias is Jack's brother.

I am gutted.

Like my stomach has been cut wide open with a blunt knife and my insides are spilling out all over the floor.

I wrap my arms around my stomach, trying to hold the hurt in. I'm afraid if I let go, it will start pouring out and never stop.

I always thought it would be Tobias who finally finished me off.

Turns out, it's the brother who will do me in.

With an invisible blade.

"He's your brother?" I don't know how I manage to speak in this moment.

"Yes."

The room tilts. The floor I'm standing on giving way beneath my feet.

I catch hold of the door to keep myself up.

Jack starts coming over to me.

"Don't come near me!" I cry, putting a hand up between us.

He halts in his tracks, not coming any closer.

I press the heel of the hand not currently holding me up to my forehead, trying to gather my racing thoughts.

Lies. It was all lies. Every touch. Every word he said.

Everything was a goddamn lie. And I fell for it, like the idiot I am.

I just went in blindly. Trustingly. Letting my feelings for him lead me. I stopped listening to my own rules.

I deserve everything that is happening to me right now.

I stare across the room at him. "Ho-how … wh-why …" I don't even know what I'm asking. What I actually want answers to.

Does it really matter?

No.

He's Tobias's brother, and that is all I need to know.

Which means, I need to get out of here. Away from him.

My keys to my apartment are in my bag. As are my rape alarm and mace.

Which is on the floor, next to the sofa. Behind where Jack is standing.

Fuck.

"Are you going to hurt me?"

He looks stunned. Like I'm the one who just dropped the mother of all bombs in here. "Of course not. No. I never could. Audrey—"

"I'm leaving," I cut him off before he can say any more. "I am going to walk past you and get my bag. And then I'm leaving."

"No. Audrey, please. We need to talk about this—"

"No!" A burst of anger flies out of me. "What I need to do is get far away from you."

"You have to let me explain."

"I don't need to do a single thing! Except for get out of here."

Jack stares at me for what feels like forever.

I can see guilt in his eyes. But that guilt means nothing.

Nothing.

Because I know he would do it to me all over again. Use me again like he has been doing.

He is only feeling guilty because he got caught.

Jesus. How long would he have kept lying to me? Sleeping with me?

I feel sick.

Jack turns away from me and picks up my bag from the floor.

I watch his every move, ready to attack or flee, whichever becomes necessary.

He takes a couple of steps toward me. I tense up.

Then, he stretches his arm out, holding my bag out to me.

I swallow hard. Forcing my feet to move, I quickly step forward, getting only as close to him as necessary. The man I could never seem to get close enough to, and now, I want to be as far away from him as humanly possible.

Reaching out, I snatch my bag from him and clutch it to my chest.

"Audrey, we have to talk. This isn't right. That picture—"

"Stop talking!" I cry.

I can feel my eyes filling with his betrayal.

Heart pounding, I turn away from him, refusing to let him see my tears.

I've already opened the door, and I'm walking through it when he says in a low voice, "I am sorry, Audrey. I never meant … for this."

I pause for a second, keeping my back to him.

Then, I just slam the door on his words. So hard that the drywall rattles.

Running to my apartment, I dig in my bag for my keys, blinking away the stupid tears threatening to fall.

Finally, I find them and let myself in, and then I lock the door behind me, sliding all the dead bolts into place.

I slump back against the door and then slide down it until my ass hits the floor. Bringing my knees up to my chest, I wrap my arms around them. Let my head fall to them.

And I allow the tears to silently run down my legs.

TWENTY-EIGHT

"Audrey."

The sound of Jack's deep yet soft voice on the other side of my door jolts me awake.

I don't know how long I've been sitting here, but my ass is numb, my legs are stiff, and the tears I was crying have dried on my face.

Even though everything aches, I don't move, afraid he'll hear me.

I hear him sigh. It sounds sad.

I hate that my heart reaches for him. Stupid, dumb heart.

How can I still feel anything for him?

I let myself be vulnerable with Jack. I showed him the worst part of me, and he betrayed me. In the worst possible way.

"Audrey … I know you're there." His words are tentative. "I can hear you breathing through the door."

I instantly hold my breath even though it's pointless because, like he said, he knows I'm here.

"Look …" he exhales the word. "You don't have to say anything … just listen to what I have to say. Please."

I say nothing.

He must take my silence as my acceptance.

It's not that I want to listen to him. But moving from this spot doesn't seem doable either.

"I'm sorry I lied. No … that's wrong. I'm not sorry. Because if I hadn't lied, I would never have gotten to know you, and for that, I will never be sorry."

Tears start to pool in the corners of my eyes again.

"But I am sorry for the way you found out. It should have come from me. And I wanted to tell you. I just didn't know how. As time went on, it got …" Another sigh. "I knew I would lose you the moment I told you, and I wasn't ready for that … I don't know if I ever will be." I hear his intake of breath. "Audrey … I need you to know that being with you … the way I feel about you … that was never a lie."

A tear runs down my face.

"I came here … because …"

Why, Jack? Why did you come here? Why did you do this to me? I was fine until you came here and turned my life upside down.

Another sigh. "Toby didn't kill those women, Audrey."

The way he calls him Toby. With familiarity.

Because he is his family.

His brother.

The thought makes me feel violently sick.

"It wasn't him who hurt you that night. I know the evidence pointed his way … but I *know* my brother. It wasn't him. And I came here … because you were here. I knew the real killer would follow you here. You were …"

His reason for killing.

He doesn't say the words. He doesn't have to.

"An obsession like that doesn't just stop overnight. I knew he would follow you here. I came ... not expecting ... *you*. It is true; I wanted to get close to you, become friendly, so I could ... I don't know. Get some insight. Find out who was in your life. See if anyone was watching you. Following you. I just didn't fucking expect ..."

What, Jack?

Another deep exhale. "You, Audrey. I didn't expect you."

He sounds defeated.

"I didn't expect this between us. To feel the way I do every time I look at you ... like ... I ..."

Like you ... what?

Another sigh. I hear movement. A rustle. I can just imagine his hand dragging through his hair the way it does when he can't find the words he wants to say.

"For a guy whose words make him a living, I am doing a shitty job at expressing what I feel." A sad-sounding laugh leaves him. "I'm crazy about you, Audrey. When I'm around you ... I feel alive in a way I haven't in a really long time. And I know I lied and that I am the last person you want to trust right now. But it's the truth. How I feel about you.

"And I didn't put that picture in my wallet. I'm not the kind of guy who carries photos around in his wallet. And I'm also not that stupid. Forgive me for saying this, but I told you that I wasn't ready for you to know who I was, and that was the reality of the situation. So, no way would I risk having anything that would cause you to find out.

"When I came here, I brought nothing here with me to link me to Toby in any way. And I definitely did not put a printed-out newspaper photo in my wallet.

"I know you don't want to listen to me or hear what I'm saying, but you need to. Someone planted that picture there. Which means, whether you want to believe it or not, that I was right … the real killer is here, and he wants me gone. And that means, we're both in danger."

TWENTY-NINE

I don't know why I open the door.

Maybe it's because he said we're in danger, and that has been a fear of mine. A worry of a copycat. Especially with the recent murders.

Maybe I open it because something in the back of my brain wonders if what he said could have merit. He seemed really convincing when he said that he didn't put the picture in his wallet. I would like to say that I know when Jack is lying, but clearly, I don't.

I never really knew him at all. Not even a little bit.

But I'm also not dumb enough to not see the logic in what he's saying about him not wanting me to know who he was, so why would he carry a picture there in his wallet? And then tell me to get the money out of it to pay for dinner?

He could have forgotten.

No. Jack is a lot of things. Mainly a liar. But a stupid man he is not.

He was clever enough to find me and follow me here.

Maybe I open the door because I have questions. Now that I've calmed a little, I have questions I need him to answer.

I could have asked through the door.

Or maybe I open the damn door because I'm in love with him. And people do blind, irresponsible shit when they're in love. Even things that could get them killed.

Jack is on his feet. Staring at me.

I can't even imagine what I look like right now.

He looks wrung out. His hair is messed up from running his hands through it, I assume.

But still beautiful.

Always beautiful.

I hate that.

I hate him.

And I hate even more that I don't hate him, not really.

"I'm sorry—" he starts in a soft voice.

"Don't," I cut him off, my voice arctic. "I have questions. I want you to answer them."

"Anything," he tells me, the look on his face earnest. Not that I can trust any way Jack looks anymore.

"And I want the truth," I add. "All of it."

"Everything I have told you from the moment I met you has been the truth. Except for Tobias. Keeping who he is to me, that is the only thing I have ever held back from you."

I wrap my arms around myself, needing to stop my heart from reaching out to him. My idiot, traitorous heart.

"And your ex-girlfriend." The words spill out of my mouth before I can stop them. And it's a damn stupid thing to say at such a serious time as this.

Jack frowns. "What ex-girlfriend?"

"It doesn't matter."

"What ex-girlfriend, Audrey?" His voice is firmer.

I shift on my feet. "The friend in Australia. You were weird every time you mentioned him, so I figured it was an ex." An important ex-girlfriend.

His expression shifts to guilt again. I feel like I'm going to get used to seeing this expression. "I was talking about Toby. He was the one who sent my manuscript off. When I said it, I knew I had dug myself into a hole, so I panicked and just said it was an old friend."

I think back to that moment in the restaurant, and it all makes sense.

There I was, feeling this pathetic jealousy, thinking it was an ex-girlfriend, and he was actually talking about his brother. The man who is in prison for stalking, kidnapping, and physically assaulting me. Oh, and also murdering multiple women.

I feel sick again.

I turn from him and walk into the kitchen. I get a bottle of water from the fridge and gulp some down. I don't bother to offer him a drink.

I'm not exactly feeling hospitable at the moment.

I look over at him. He's still standing in the open doorway.

"You can come in."

"Are you sure?"

"We can't exactly have this conversation with the door open for the neighbors to hear. I'm sure they have heard enough already."

"I just want you to feel comfortable. Safe."

"Are you going to hurt me?"

He holds my eyes. "No."

"Then, come in and close the door. But just so you know, I have a rape alarm and mace in my bag. And a drawer full of kitchen utensils that can serve as weapons."

Jack leans back against the door he just closed. "Noted. You've also got a mean right hook, if I remember right."

His lips lift into a small smile, but I am in no mood to take a stroll down memory lane with him right now.

"You said you had questions …" he prompts when I don't say anything.

I do have questions, but trying to gather them up and get them in any sort of order is feeling impossible right now.

"So, you know my surname isn't actually Hayes? That it's Irwin." I start with something small. I can work my way up to the big stuff.

Jack nods in response.

"And am I right in assuming that your real surname is Ripley, not Canti?"

"No. It is Canti. When I said that I only kept that Toby is my brother from you, that was the truth. Toby and I have different fathers. That's why we have different surnames."

I guess that's why I don't see a similarity between them. Not that all siblings necessarily look the same. Cole and I don't.

"My mom and dad divorced when I was a kid," he explains. "And Toby's dad was an asshole. He ran off when Tobias was a few weeks old. I was eleven when he was born. I pretty much helped my mom raise him."

"So, the small part of your past that you gave to me, that was all true. The military. The writing."

"Yes. And you weren't exactly forthcoming on your past either, Audrey."

"And now, I know why you didn't push the issue." I laugh humorlessly. "And there I was, thinking you just weren't a pushy guy."

Jack says nothing. There's just that guilt lining his eyes, which has been there since I found that damn photograph.

"Why did I not recognize you? I knew your mom from the trial. You weren't there. I would have remembered."

"The military wouldn't let me leave to come home for the trial. When your brother's on trial for murder and kidnapping, they don't look upon that favorably to give you time off."

"Don't forget stalking and assault," I add bitterly. I absentmindedly press my hand to my scars.

"It wasn't him, Audrey," he says the words softly.

"The evidence said otherwise."

"Audrey—"

"The jury of twelve men and women all found him guilty."

"And not a single drop of DNA matched his."

"So, he was careful. A lot of killers are."

Jack sighs and drags his hand through his hair. "My brother is not careful. He's not clean. I spent the best part of my life getting that kid to shower. So, to say he would keep a crime scene spotless is a stretch."

"Maybe you're the one who's stretching. You were away in the military. People change."

"Toby didn't."

"What about the evidence found in his bedroom at your mother's house? The trinkets he stole from the victims? The knife he used on them … *me*?"

"Planted."

"By who? Why would someone frame him? Come on, Jack. You seriously want to sell to me that it wasn't Tobias? That some other person murdered these women? Stalked me? Kidnapped me? And then framed Tobias? Then, tell me who. Give me a reason."

He holds my eyes. "I don't have one. I don't know who the killer is. I just know that Toby is innocent."

"I think you want to believe he is."

He shakes his head. "I know it wasn't him. He is not a killer."

"We never really know anyone." I give him a pointed look.

"True. But I watched my brother save a bird from the neighbor's cat a year before the murders started. He nursed it back to health. Jesus, when he was five, I sat with him while he cried himself to sleep after he accidentally killed a butterfly."

I pause at his words.

"A man who does that would not kill animals and leave them on your doorstep, and he most definitely would not kill another human being."

"I … that means nothing."

"I spoke to him that night. The night you were taken. On the phone."

"I don't believe you."

"It was the home phone. I called, he answered, and I spoke to him for eleven minutes."

"What you're saying right now proves nothing!" I fire back at him.

"I have proof, Audrey. I can show you the call log from the phone company."

"They would have said in the trial …"

"It was dismissed as evidence. Yes, the call logs show a call was made to my mother's house. That it connected and that I spoke to someone for eleven minutes—right in the middle of the time you were being held—but it doesn't prove who I was talking to."

"You could have been talking to your mother."

"But I wasn't. She was sleeping. She was sick in bed."

I know this. It was all said at trial. But nothing about the phone call.

"I am telling you, Audrey. I spoke to him that night. He was home. He wasn't there with you."

"So what if you did speak to him!" I'm getting agitated. "That means nothing! He could have left and …"

I stop my words because he didn't leave me that night. He was there, in my apartment. I was tied up and blindfolded. I couldn't see him. But I could hear him. Moving around that room. But even if he hadn't moved a muscle for those horrific hours, I would have known he was there. I could *feel* him there, watching me.

"But he didn't leave, did he?" Jack's eyes are focused wholly on me. "You said in your testimony that whoever was in your room with you, he never left you alone, not even for a second. From the moment he broke into your apartment until the moment he left, he was there with you the whole time." Jack takes a measured step toward me. "You never saw his face. Never heard his voice. It could have been anyone." Another step closer. "*Anyone*, Audrey."

"The knife was found in his room!" I can feel panic at the memory of that night. The fear I felt pouring into my blood, poisoning my veins. "It was covered in my blood! The same knife that killed all of those women."

Jack stays where he stands. His face is resolute. He believes what he says ... thinks. "It was put there by the real killer."

"No!" I yell. I cover my face with my hands.

Why is he doing this to me?

I'm shaking so badly.

I'm hurt and angry. I don't know what to do with these feelings ... it's too much.

I want ...

I don't know what I want.

I suddenly feel tired. Drained. Exhausted. I just want to go to sleep. Forget about all of this.

I drag my hands down from my face, feeling weary. "What do you want from me, Jack?"

His expression softens. "I don't want anything from you, Audrey. No, that's not true. I do want something from you ... you. I want you."

"You didn't come here for me. You came here for your brother."

"That is true. I came here because I wanted to find the person who had put my brother in jail. You were the only link I had to help make that happen. I just didn't expect to ..."

"What?" My laugh is bitter. "You didn't expect to want to fuck me?"

"Love you," he says. "I didn't expect to fall in love with you."

Those words pierce me harder and hurt so much more than anything else he's said so far.

"You need to leave."

"Audrey ... *please.*"

"Leave!" I cry.

His shoulders slump. "I can't."

"Why? Because you think that I'm the key to your brother's freedom? News flash: I'm not. I think he did it! And nothing you say can change my mind."

I'm hurt and confused. Misery has lodged itself into my throat. "What are you going to do? Hold me hostage like Tobias did?"

Jack looks appalled. "No. Of course not. But I can't leave you alone either."

I open my mouth to speak, but Jack cuts me off, "It's not safe for you here, Audrey. That picture was put in my wallet. I will swear on whatever you want me to, so you'll believe me when I say that it's not mine. Meaning someone put it there. Whether you believe that Tobias is guilty or not is irrelevant right now. Someone wanted you to know who I was—"

"Maybe a decent person who thought I had a right to know the truth."

"Then, why access my private property and plant the picture in my wallet? Why not just give it to you? A decent person would do that. No, someone wanted you to find it. They wanted to drive us apart. Why? I'd say it was so you'd be alone."

"I was alone for months before I even met you. Nothing happened."

"Not true. Murders have happened. The guy at your work and his girlfriend. Those women who were killed before I even got here."

I'm staring at him, unsure of what to say.

"The dead rat in your apartment."

A cold feeling washes over me. "That was nothing."

"You know it wasn't. I don't know what's happening here. What the end game is. But I know it includes you. It always circles back to you."

"It always circles back to you."

"You're not safe here, Audrey."

"Maybe I'm not safe because of you. Or with you." I'm so tired. I'm surprised I'm even still able to stand.

"I won't ever hurt you, Audrey. I never would."

"But you already have," I say quietly.

The silence hanging between us is fraught and heavy. And what he said is penetrating.

I might not believe that Tobias is innocent like Jack does. But that doesn't mean he's wrong about there being someone else involved. Or even a copycat. Like I've feared all along. Someone watching and waiting. To finish off what was started.

"So ... if I'm not safe here, then what do I do?"

"Leave here. With me. I can take you someplace safe until we can figure this out."

"Or I could go to the police."

"And tell them what? That someone put a picture in my wallet?"

Okay. So, he has a point. But even still ...

"I'm not going anywhere with you, Jack. I don't trust you."

He sighs. "I know I'm the last person you want to be around at the moment—and with good reason. But being alone is not a good idea for you right now either. I have a safe place I can take you. It's a cabin up in the mountains—"

"I can keep myself safe, thanks. No way in hell am I staying in a cabin in the mountains with you."

Truth is, I don't know if I can keep myself safe. I couldn't the last time. I have nowhere to go. It's not like I can go back to Chicago. I would only be putting Cole at risk if I did. But a cabin up in the mountains with Jack isn't an option either.

"Do you own a gun?" Jack asks me out of nowhere.

I frown. "No."

I hate guns. I hate any kind of weapons. Hence why I have never carried one. Only ever my can of mace and my rape alarm.

"Then, you can't keep yourself safe."

My arms fold across my chest. "I don't need a gun to do that."

"Self-defense will only get you so far."

He does have a point. But still …

"Do you have a … gun?" I ask warily.

"Yes," he says slowly, seemingly gauging my reaction. "And it can keep us both safe."

Sighing, I walk over on wobbly legs and sit down heavily on the sofa. I shake my head. "I can't leave with you. Firstly, I don't trust you—kind of a big one. And secondly, the only thing triggering this is a photo in your wallet, which you say was planted."

"It was." He takes a seat on the coffee table, putting him in front of me.

I can smell the mint from the soap he used in the shower that he took not so long ago. Even though it feels like a lifetime ago.

He's become a different person to me in such a short period of time.

Yet I still feel exactly the same about him.

It's confusing.

If, an hour ago, he had sat here, asking me to go on a trip with him, I would have said yes without hesitation.

But he is also not the Jack I knew from an hour ago.

And he is most definitely not asking me to go away for the weekend with him.

He's asking me to go into hiding with him from a mystery person who might not even exist. Based solely on the fact that a picture was put in his wallet.

"I think you're overreacting about this, Jack. I really do."

"And I get why you think that. Because you think the real killer is behind bars. I know he's not. I was worried about your safety, Audrey, but nothing has happened to you since you moved here, aside from finding that dead rat in your apartment, so I figured you were safe for now. This photo in my wallet changes everything. Someone wants you away from me. That might not put you in immediate danger, but it means something is happening, and I'm not willing to put your safety at risk."

"Maybe if I just stay away from you, that will solve all of my problems," I say the words with all the anger I feel inside of me.

Jack sighs. It sounds defeated. "Okay. Just promise me … you'll be careful. And if anything happens—"

"Then, I'll call the police first."

The hurt in his eyes causes an ache in my chest to bloom.

I hate that I have feelings for him. It makes this so much harder.

Jack nods. It's a final kind of nod.

It splinters something inside of me. But I let it fragment, and when he gets up and leaves my apartment, I don't stop him. Even though my tortured heart is crying for him to stay.

THIRTY

A shadow.

I jump out of sleep. Bolting upright. Heart beating like crazy in my chest.

I hate it when I have those nightmares. *He's* always there. I just can't ever see his face. Always a shadow.

I press a hand to my chest and try to steady my heart and breaths.

Mouth dry, I get out of bed and go to the kitchen to get a glass of water.

As I'm walking, the memories of yesterday flood me. Finding out who Jack is. Who his brother is …

I'm still struggling to believe it.

But really, I shouldn't be surprised. I have no luck in life. Only bad Karma finds me. Over and over.

The worst thing is that I miss Jack.

I hate knowing that he is just down the hall in his apartment, sleeping, and I'm here, alone, without him.

Could we get past this?

Could I?

I won't deny that a part of me wants to. But I don't see how we could.

Considering his brother is in prison, partly for crimes committed against me.

The thought of all of this brings an ache to my chest. I don't want to think about it. I can't. So, I do what I do best. I box up all thoughts of Jack and pack them away in my mind.

I get a glass from the cupboard and the water from the fridge, and then I pour myself a drink.

I take a sip.

I feel restless. I know I won't get any more sleep tonight.

If Jack were here—

Stop.

Sighing, I sit down on the sofa. I look at the book on the coffee table. It has been so long since I read a book.

I have been too busy with—

Nope.

I put my glass of water down and pick the book up. I open it up. The words on the page blur into one.

"Great. I can't even read now." I slap the pages of the book together and toss it onto the coffee table.

And knock the glass of water over.

"Shit!"

The water is running off the table onto the floor.

Just fucking great.

Righting the now-empty glass, I jog to the kitchen and grab the paper towels from the cupboard.

Taking it back with me, I stare down at the mess.

It's everywhere.

Fuck my life.

Bending down, I start mopping up the water.

I didn't know a glass could hold so much damn water.

I'm on my hands and knees, mopping the floor up.

Christ.

It's gone under the sofa.

I slip a hand under, trying to wipe it dry, but it's run too far for me to reach.

I'm going to have to move the sofa.

Ugh. I really should have stayed in bed.

I put my hands on the base of the sofa and give it a firm shove back. It moves back a bit.

Another shove. It goes back farther this time now that I've got some momentum going.

A bit farther back, and I'll be able to clean this mess up.

One. Two. Three.

I give it a big shove.

It slides back easily.

Bingo.

I grab some fresh paper towels, and on my hands and knees again, I start wiping the water up.

As I move around on the floor, one of the floorboards shifts. Pushes down at one side under my weight, the other side coming up.

Oh great. A loose floorboard.

I'll have to get the super to fix it.

I bet the water has trickled down through the gap. I get some more towels and wipe around the loose board, making sure it's dry before I push it back into place.

Light glinting on something silver catches my eye through the gap in the floorboard.

What is that?

The imaginative reader in me has a brief fantasy of finding buried treasure under here.

Under a floorboard in an apartment. Yeah, sure, Audrey.

It's more likely that a coin dropped under here or a nail came out of the floorboard.

Curious, I put my fingertip under the lip of the floorboard and ease it up.

It comes up easier than I expected it to.

Lifting it free, I pause with it in my hand when I see what's lying beneath my floor.

A knife.

Next to it is a stained cloth.

My heart starts to beat faster. The stains look like blood.

And there's a blue velvet jewelry pouch.

It reminds me of the one my mother used to keep her pearls in.

Pulse beating in my ears, I reach down and pick up the pouch.

Pulling the string open, I look inside.

There are two rings, a necklace, a bracelet, and a man's wristwatch.

"What the hell is this?" I whisper to myself.

I sense movement in the corner of my eye.

Spinning my head around, I stifle a scream.

Relief replaces fear when I see who it is. Even if I am confused as to why he's here.

"Jesus, Cole!" I exclaim to my brother, pressing my hand to my chest, covering my thudding heart. "You just scared ten years off my life."

Cole steps around from behind me and kneels on the floor in front of me. His knees just touching mine. But he doesn't say anything.

"What are you doing here? How did you find me?" My head swivels to my closed front door. "How did you get in?"

He still says nothing.

I stare at him. He looks tired. His hair is unkempt. His clothes are wrinkled.

Which is strange because Cole is always impeccable. His hair is always neatly combed. Clothes always ironed.

And he's acting strange. I mean, Cole is often weird. But this sudden appearance in my apartment and this overly long, stretching silence are odd, even for him.

"Cole? Answer me."

Nothing. His eyes are looking down at the things I've found.

"They were in my floor," I tell him. "I spilled some water and found these beneath a loose floorboard under the sofa. There's jewelry in this pouch. Don't you think it looks like the one Mom used to keep her pearls in? And I'm pretty sure that's blood on that cloth."

Cole sighs. Finally, a response comes from him. "You weren't supposed to find these, Audrey."

"What?" I laugh, but it's a nervous sound. Something doesn't feel right. "What do you mean, I wasn't supposed to find these? You're acting really weird, Cole. You never answered my question as to what you're doing here. I never told you where I lived. So, how did you know where to find me?"

"I always know where you are, Audrey."

I'm staring at him, and I have this alien feeling. Fear. I have never once felt that around Cole. He has always been my protector. He's always taken care of me. He would never hurt me. But right now ... I'm not so sure.

"Cole, you're scaring me. What's going on?"

The expression on his face is sad. He takes the pouch from my hand and puts it back into the floor where I found it, next to the knife and stained cloth.

Cole reaches for my hand. It's shaking. So hard that I can barely feel his hand touching mine. His fingers entwine with mine. I stare down at them.

What is happening here? Why can't I feel him?

"It's time, Audrey."

I blink up at him. My vision goes hazy. "Time for what?" I hear myself saying.

"For you to rest."

Then, he moves so fast that I don't have time to react.

And then it's just blackness.

THIRTY-ONE

Cole

I hate to do this.

I don't want to hurt Audrey.

I never want to hurt her.

But I don't have a choice.

She wasn't supposed to find those things. My things. My private things.

She was never meant to know about any of this.

But she found them, leaving me with no other option.

I know Audrey. She would have overthought things. Thought about the maybes and whys. She would have thought of the recent murders. And then she would have taken them to Jack, and he would have told her to take them to the police. Because he would have thought that they might be able to help get his brother out of jail.

And he would have been right.

So, they have to go.

Just like last time.

Although, the last time, when I had to frame Tobias for the murders, it was because the police were beginning to get suspicious.

In the beginning, they had seen Audrey as a victim. But as time went on, I could tell their thoughts were beginning to change. They were starting to wonder if maybe Audrey had actually played a part in the murders.

I couldn't have that.

I needed to point their scent another way.

And Tobias—poor, stupid Tobias who lived down the street and had a crush on Audrey—was perfect.

But now, it's Audrey, not the police, who has left me with no other choice.

I walk over to the kitchen, get some disposable gloves from the drawer, and put them on.

Laying out some paper towels on the floor, I pick up the knife and cleaning cloth and place them on the pouch of jewelry—my small souvenirs from my victims.

None of my DNA or fingerprints are on any of these. I'm always careful to keep my things free of anything that can be traced back to me. But now, Audrey has touched the velvet pouch.

I sigh. I tip the jewelry out onto a paper towel and put the knife and cleaning cloth with them. Then, I put the pouch back into the floor and put the floorboard back in place.

I wrap the items up in a paper towel and get to my feet, bringing them with me.

Then, I push the sofa back into its original spot.

I get the key to Jack's apartment from Audrey's bag. A spare key that he gave to her.

I let myself out of the apartment, and on silent feet, I walk down the empty hallway toward Jack's apartment.

Using the key, I slide it into the lock and turn. The click of it unlocking sounds so loud in the silence of the night.

Steadying my breathing, I turn the handle and quietly open the door.

Slipping inside, I carefully close the door behind me.

His apartment is in darkness. Only the moonlight through the window providing any light.

I fucking hate this guy.

I discovered who he was totally by accident. I was online, looking him up. I needed to know all about Jack Canti. The man Audrey was allowing to fuck her, use her like a whore, and she was starting to have real feelings for him. Believing his lies. Thinking that she loved him. I couldn't allow that.

When I found out exactly who he was related to ... well, it was like a gift from God.

Audrey needed to know, of course. I knew she wouldn't have anything more to do with him once she did.

Because she always believes everything that I lay out for her to believe.

It was the only way. It has only ever been this way.

Audrey cannot cope with the truth.

And if she hadn't found my things tonight, I would have left Jack alone. So long as she stayed away from him.

I know it will hurt Audrey for me to do this, but there's no other way.

Silently, I move through Jack's apartment, looking for a place to *hide* my things. Somewhere easily findable for the police. But not so easy that it looks planted.

Because poor Jack Canti is about to be framed for my crimes.

When I'm done, the police will believe that Jack came here to finish off what his brother started—to kill Audrey.

Not that I'll kill her, of course. I could never kill Audrey.

But I will have to hurt her again.

I don't like that I have to. Just like I didn't the last time when I cut open her skin.

I walk over to the window and check to see if the sill is movable, if I can put these things here.

But, no, it's fixed down good.

Fucking Christ.

Light flashes on, momentarily blinding me.

I spin around to see Jack standing in the entrance to the living room, a gun in his hand, pointed in my direction.

I hold my breath as Jack blinks. His angry expression morphs quickly to surprise and then instantly relaxes.

"Jesus, Audrey." He lowers the gun, shoving a hand through his hair. "You frightened the shit out of me. What are you doing here? Are you okay?"

I put the items down behind me on the sill.

And then I smile.

THIRTY-TWO

Cole

Jack moves through the living room, coming toward me. He puts the gun into the waistband at the back of his sleep pants while he walks.

I track the movement with my eyes. Before looking back to his face.

A face filled with concern.

I would actually feel bad for the guy if I didn't dislike him so much.

What Audrey sees in him, I will never know.

I just need to figure out how to handle this situation.

My hands are still behind my back. Gloves are still on. The knife is wrapped in the paper towel. I quickly peel the gloves off and shove them down the back of the shorts that I'm wearing.

My fingers fumble to free the knife. Not that it'll do me much good against his gun. I manage to loosen the towel from around it just as Jack reaches me.

"Did something happen?" he asks me.

He's worried for her. I'm sure Audrey would find it sweet.

I just find it irritating.

I shake my head.

He's staring at me. "You sure? You seem"—his brow furrows in concentration—"different."

"Different."

I have to suppress a smile.

If only he knew just how different I was.

I don't say anything. If I do speak, Jack will know that I'm not Audrey straightaway. Our voices differ. I can mimic Audrey's, but to someone close to her, they would know the difference.

As much as I might dislike it, Jack is close to my sister.

And he's also smart.

What I need to do right now is get that gun off him.

And there's only one way to do it. Distraction.

Lifting a hand, I press it to his chest.

His breathing stutters.

So fucking easy.

I press my lips to his and kiss him.

Not exactly what I want to do right now—or anytime ever, to be perfectly honest—but needs must.

And I will do whatever is necessary.

Jack kisses me back. I can feel him losing himself in the kiss.

Good. I need him distracted for just long enough.

Reaching a hand back, I locate my knife with my fingers. Curling them around it, I pick it up, holding it in my right hand, while I move my left hand, slipping it down the skin of his back.

When I locate his gun, I wrap my fingers around the handle, and then in one swift movement, I pull it from his waistband and bring my arm holding the knife from behind my back. I turn it upward and plunge the blade into his neck.

The look of shock and confusion and anguish on his face is one that I will remember for a little while at least.

I do almost feel sorry for the bastard.

Almost.

But he was only fucking Audrey to get close to her, so he could free his stupid brother from prison.

He hurt Audrey. So, I don't feel too bad about killing him.

And it's not like I had any other choice.

Neither he nor Audrey left me another option.

Audrey will be upset though when she finds out that he's dead.

But I'll deal with that when the time comes.

Jack staggers back from me. His hands clutching his throat. His back hits the wall, and he slides down it until he's sitting, slumped on the floor.

And I watch him.

The way the blood seeps out from between his fingers. Running down his chest.

Jack won't die just yet. He's got a few minutes. Maybe more. I didn't hit a major vein when I stuck the knife in him. Because I didn't want to.

He'll bleed out slowly. Which is just how I like it.

This is my favorite part.

"Au-dr-ey … wh-wh-why?" The words are quiet and garbled. He can't shout or yell for help because of the blood flooding his throat and his lungs.

"Audrey isn't here at the moment."

He hears it. The difference in our voices. I see it in his confused and fearful eyes.

And I am enjoying every single second of this.

It's what I live for.

Of course, I live for Audrey too.

But this … the killing … this is for me.

"How about I tell you a little story?"

I take a few steps backward and rest my ass on the arm of the sofa. Jack's gun in one hand, my knife in my other.

"Once upon a time, there was a little girl called Audrey, and she had a brother called Cole. Their father was a mean, cruel bastard who used to beat on his wife and kids. Cole would protect Audrey as best he could because that's what older brothers do—they protect their younger sibling.

"One day, when Audrey was four and Cole was eight, their dad was in a particularly bad mood. A terrible mood in fact. Their mother was in the kitchen, cooking dinner. Cole and Audrey were in the back closet that led into the kitchen. When they had to be in the house, they would play in there to stay out of the way of their father.

"They heard arguing begin in the kitchen and then the sounds of their father hitting their mother. Cole told Audrey to cover her ears. That it would all be fine. But it wasn't fine. Not that day. The sound that came from their mother … was unnatural. Cole knew something bad was happening. He looked through the slats in the door, and he could see blood. Blood running across the floor. He told Audrey to stay there, and he walked into the kitchen. Cole saw his mother's body on the floor, surrounded by blood. He screamed. So, his father made Cole stop screaming. Then, their father took the knife to his own throat and slit it wide open.

"Audrey always did what Cole told her to, and she didn't leave that closet. She stayed there for three days until a worried neighbor called the police because she hadn't seen the family for a few days and there was a bad smell coming from the house.

"Audrey had no other family. So, she was placed with a good Christian family. Dorothy and Patrick Irwin went on to adopt her. Only Patrick and Dorothy weren't good people. Patrick liked to rape little girls, and Dorothy turned a blind eye, allowing him to.

"What Cole hadn't realized was that Audrey had seen her family slaughtered that day. Cole told her to cover her ears in that moment in the closet but not to close her eyes. His one mistake. And through the slats in that door, she saw *everything*. And then she had been left all alone … to live with those monsters.

"Audrey cried for Cole every single night after that bastard made her do things no child ever should. Begged for him to come back and save her. So, that's what I did. I came back and protected her, like I always had tried to. Only I wouldn't fail her ever again. So, every night, when that sick fuck she had to now call father would come into her bedroom to take what he wanted from her, Audrey would simply fall asleep, and I would take her place."

"Do-n't un-der-stand." Blood spatters down from his mouth and onto his pants.

It's like artwork.

My beautifully made canvas.

"You wouldn't." I shake my head at him, feeling irritated. "I am Audrey. And she is me." I point at my chest.

"Wh-ere … Au-dr-ey?"

"She's resting at the moment. At times, Audrey sees me as if I were standing in front of her. And other times … like now, she sleeps, and it's just me. She has no idea that we coexist in the same body. And she doesn't need to. It works better for both of us that way. I had to take over because she'd found my things." I gesture with the knife to the other items on the windowsill. "And I knew that Audrey would try to do the right thing. Because that's Audrey. She's a good person."

"Mur-ders … you."

"Yes. All me." I smile. "The murders in Chicago that your brother is sitting pretty in prison for right now. And I know what you're thinking … *Why him?*" I shrug. "He was an easy target. He had a stupid crush on Audrey, and she had no clue he existed. But I did though. I knew. I know everything. And the police investigating the murders were getting suspicious. They were starting to ask Audrey too many questions. It had been my error to link them to her in the first place. So, I had to take the direction away from Audrey and me. And you have to know, cutting her that night, terrorizing her, it wasn't something I wanted to do, but I had no choice. I had to sell the idea that it was Tobias. It was the only way.

"I'd killed her adoptive parents as well." While I'm here, I might as well give him full disclosure. Not like he's going to be able to tell anyone, and I'm enjoying my little story time.

"Although I didn't get to have as much fun with them as I wanted. But I did get the most pleasure from killing those two. And I know you're probably thinking, *Why didn't you kill them years ago?* And the answer is, I didn't know I could." I shrug. "Wasn't sure I was capable of it. But turns out, I am, and I'm damn fucking good at it.

"You see, when Audrey left for college, I figured it was over with that sicko. But when she graduated, she didn't have a job to go to. No money to fall back on. So, she went back home. To that fucking house. And it started again. He started raping her again … well, me. Because it's always me." My hand curls tight around the handle of the knife. "So, I decided to make it stop. Only wish I could have cut him open like the pig he was. But it would have been too messy. Too many questions. The cops would have looked straight at Audrey. It's always the family they look at first, and Audrey was set to inherit everything—the house and money. So, I … tampered with their car one night before they went out for dinner. Millions of people die in automobile accidents every day.

"Annoying thing was that Audrey wasn't happy they were dead. She actually mourned them. But that was my error. I had protected her, shielded her from everything, so she never really knew who they were." I sigh. "She was just so sad. Honestly, it was starting to bug me. So, I decided to try and cheer her up. I left her notes. Little gifts. To make her feel special. Let her think she had an admirer. But it didn't work. She was still fucking depressed.

"There was this bird that used to sit outside her bedroom window; it used to chirp nonstop. Honestly, it was like nails on a blackboard. I thought getting rid of that would make her happy. And it was fun, snapping its little neck. The cat next door was shitting all over the flowers in the garden. I knew it bothered her. So, I killed the cat. But she was still fucking sad.

"Then, one day, Audrey seemed to be perking up. She actually went out to get her hair done. And the bitch at the salon was awful to her. Some stuck-up receptionist who made her feel like an inconvenience. Audrey went home and cried. I was so fucking mad. It was the first day that she'd actually started to feel better, and that bitch brought her back down.

"So, later on that night, when it was dark and Audrey was resting, I took a knife with me and went back to the salon ... followed that receptionist cunt to her house ... and made her feel *bad* for a while until she stopped feeling anything at all. I left a note for Audrey, letting her know it was a present for her. Not like I could take the body home and leave it on the doorstep for her. It wasn't until later, when I saw it in the press, that she looked like Audrey. Weird, right? But I kind of liked it too. It felt good. And we all need a little something for ourselves, right?"

I look over at Jack, realizing I got a little lost in my own story.

And he's dead.

Ah, shame.

I missed watching him take his last breath.

I do enjoy that part. Almost as much as watching the blood ... the life seep out of them.

Oh well. That's what I get for talking too much about myself. You live and learn.

Sighing, I stand and tuck the knife in the front waistband of the sleep shorts I'm wearing. I go to the kitchen, put the gun down, and wash Jack's blood off my hands. Then, taking the gun with me, I go to Jack's bedroom. I clean it up with my clothes, getting rid of any blood or fingerprints that might be on it, and then put the gun in the drawer in his nightstand.

I return to the living room and get the bloody cloth and jewelry off the windowsill. I glance around for a place they could have been *hidden* when *Audrey* accidentally discovered them.

I see a high cupboard in the kitchen.

I take the jewelry and cloth with me. Reach up on my tiptoes and open the cupboard.

It has some paperwork and a first aid box.

Perfect.

I grab hold of the first aid box and carry it over to the coffee table. Placing it down, I open it up. Shifting things around, I put the jewelry and cloth in there, leaving it open.

I remember the gloves stuffed down the back of the shorts I'm wearing. I have nowhere to put them. I can't leave them anywhere here in Jack's apartment. They're covered in my prints and DNA.

I shove them further down the shorts, into the panties I'm wearing. I'll dispose of them later.

I turn to Jack, looking at him.

I almost feel bad for this one.

Almost.

And only because I know this will hurt Audrey.

But she'll get over it.

She'll have to.

Knowing what I need to do next, I take a deep breath. Because, last time, when I cut this skin, I was doing it to Audrey, so I didn't feel a thing.

But this time, I'm cutting myself. I can't let Audrey come back right now. I have to play Audrey and see this thing through myself.

She won't accept this.

She won't understand.

I walk over to Jack's lifeless body, standing in front of it.

I see movement from the corner of my eye and notice the cat—Jack's cat—walking casually into the living room.

It stops and stares at me.

"Suppose you heard all of that. Not that you'll be telling anybody."

God, look at me, turning into Audrey, talking to a damn stupid cat.

The cat looks at me for a second longer, and then with a swish of its tail, it walks into the kitchen.

I watch it for a moment longer until it disappears behind the counter.

Then, I take the knife from my waistband and curl my hand around the handle.

Gritting my teeth, jaw clenched, I press the blade to my skin, and I start cutting.

A slash on my arm. One on my thigh.

I never got to feel this the night I cut Audrey … because it was me doing it to her.

But now, I can feel it, and it feels … amazing. Almost … cathartic.

Like a release I didn't know I needed.

I do know though that the cuts aren't going to be enough to sell this.

I need to do more.

With a hard swallow, I grip the knife handle with both hands. I press the blade to my stomach. I shut my eyes.

And plunge it into my stomach.

"Fuuuccck," I cry quietly through gritted teeth.

Water runs out from the corners of my eyes.

The knife clatters to the floor.

I press a hand to the wound and stare down at it.

Blood seeps between my fingers, turning my skin red. The hands ... body that I share with my sister.

And it's ... *incredible.*

The pain ... the blood ... my blood ... her blood ... it's exhilarating to feel and see.

I don't want the feeling to end.

But I know it has to.

Still, I allow myself a few seconds of enjoyment that I didn't know existed until this very moment ... before the show begins.

Then, I breathe in deeply, open my mouth, and start screaming.

EPILOGUE

Audrey
Eight Months Later

The bar buzzes with people all around me, people who have come in here for a drink after work, just like I've done.

The only difference is, they're in groups and couples.

And I'm alone, sitting with my back to them all, at a table by the window.

There was a time not so long ago when I wouldn't sit with my back to a room full of people.

But I've realized that it doesn't matter which way you're facing.

If someone wants to get close to you, they will.

Jack … he got close to me.

The same ache in my chest appears that I always feel when I think of him.

I press the heel of my hand against my sternum, trying to ease the hurt away.

But I know nothing will ever take away the pain of what happened.

Even though I remember very little of that night.

Only waking up and getting a glass of water. Spilling it on the floor.

And then nothing until I woke up in the hospital.

The weird part though is, I'm sure that I saw Cole that night. In my apartment.

But I know that can't be right because Cole wasn't there. He was in Chicago.

I haven't told Cole that I thought he was there.

I don't know why I haven't told him, to be honest. Every time I open my mouth to voice the words, something stops me.

Maybe it's because I know how crazy it sounds.

I can't remember Jack trying to kill me. But I have a false memory of my brother being there.

I mean, the only reason I know what happened that fateful night is because of the police.

Detectives Peters and Sparks.

They came to see me in the hospital. They wanted my version of events from that night. I told them the very little I did know, which was nothing of worth.

The whole time I spoke, Detective Sparks looked at me with this cold expression. Like he didn't believe me. Like it was me who had done something wrong.

He said nothing. Not one single word in the time he was there. It was unnerving.

It was Detective Peters who informed me that Jack was dead. That I had killed him in self-defense after he attacked me, stabbing me first. That it appeared that I had discovered that Jack was the killer of Molly Hall, Natalie Jenkins, Sarah Greenwood, and Michael King. That I had found the murder weapon—the knife he tried to kill me with—in a first aid kit in his apartment along with some of the victims' personal items.

They knew my real surname. My history with Tobias. That Jack was his older brother.

Hearing all of those words … it broke me. Knowing that Jack had been there all along to kill me. To finish what his brother had started. That I had been right in my worst fear.

Only … I *knew* Jack. I know that I am always the one to say that you never really know anyone, and that undoubtedly is true in this case.

But there's just something … deep inside of me niggling away. Bothering me. Like an itch that I can't reach.

Jack had so many opportunities to hurt me, and he never did. Not once. Until he did.

It's just … hard to piece it all together. Understand everything.

Curling my hand around my wineglass, I squeeze my eyes shut, trying to find those hidden memories. That itch in the back of my mind.

If I could just …

Stop.

I blink, shaking my head.

What was I thinking about just now?

I try to force my thought back, but it doesn't work.

I rub at my forehead, feeling an ache coming on.

My mind feels so clogged up. Clouded. Hazy.

Like the fog is so thick and I can't find my way through it.

The doctor said it was due to the trauma. That the memories from what happened that night will possibly return in the future … or they might never.

I pick my glass of wine up and take a sip, savoring the taste of it. I focus on the world through the window.

It's early evening here in Los Angeles, the sun still bright in the sky.

LA is my home now.

I left Jackson not long after I got out of the hospital. Cole said that I needed a change of scenery. That I needed to be away from all memories of Jack. It didn't take much to persuade me.

But obviously, Chicago wasn't an option for me.

Cole suggested LA. I agreed.

I had tried a small town, and that hadn't worked out. I thought maybe the sunshine might be good for me.

Cole moved here with me too.

I had been stupid to ever leave him behind like I did.

I've learned my lesson. I won't ever leave my brother again.

I need him.

Cole and I share a house in Long Beach, and I've got a job, working at a local library. I like it there. The people are nice.

I'm trying to be a little more social nowadays. Hence why I'm sitting in a bar. I force myself to come most days after work and just be around people.

Okay, I'm alone. And I wouldn't exactly say that I'm making friends. I don't think I ever will. But shutting myself off to people evidently didn't work. So, here I am.

And I have all the friends I need anyway.

Eleven lives with me now. She is the only link I have left to Jack.

I know it's stupid to still think about him after everything that happened. But I do.

Not that I would ever tell Cole this. He'd be angry with me. He thinks I adopted Eleven because I couldn't bear the thought of her not having a home. Which is the same reason that, before I left Jackson, I adopted Gary and Pork Chop, and I brought them all to LA to live with me.

Cole loves the dogs. And he likes Eleven, and she him. Which I was surprised at. Not at Eleven liking him, but Cole liking her.

I thought he'd dislike her because she was Jack's cat. But he seems to have a bond with her.

It makes me happy.

So, yeah, we definitely have a full house with those three. But I love going home to them all after a day at work. They give me purpose.

"Is anyone sitting here?"

I turn my head at the deep male voice close behind me.

The first thing I see is the suit. Tailor-made. Beer bottle in hand. Rolex around his wrist.

I lift my eyes to his face.

Tanned skin. Dark brown hair cut into a short, neat style. Brown eyes. Handsome.

Though I have no interest.

Yes …

No.

The man smiles. It's a nice smile. Easy and relaxed.

"Sorry if I'm bothering you," he says after I say nothing. "I'm just looking for a spot to sit down and enjoy my beer. It's been a long-ass day."

Yes ...

No.

"You didn't ... you're not bothering me," I answer politely.

But say no to the seat, I tell myself.

What can it hurt?

My heart is suddenly beating fast. I start to feel drowsy.

This has been happening so much recently. I've always struggled with tiredness since I was a kid. But these bouts of fatigue, they come on so quickly and from out of nowhere, making me fall asleep in random places. But the frightening thing is ... I always wake up hours later, back at home and with no clue how I got there. It's been happening regularly since I left Jackson and moved here, and it's scary as hell.

I haven't told anyone. Not even Cole.

I don't want him to worry.

But last month, it was at the bus stop when a woman took a seat on the bench beside me. The month before that, it was in a diner when I shared a booth with this nice man who had asked if he could sit at the table with me because the diner was packed.

Kind of just like what's happening now ...

I blink, staring up at the man. My vision starts to go hazy. Dark.

This isn't ... no ... I can't ... don't fall asleep.

Audrey.

Yes?

Rest now.

Cole

I blink open my eyes as I stretch out, taking full control, putting Audrey to rest.

God, that feels so much better.

Smiling easily, I pat a hand on the seat of the empty chair beside me. "The seat is all yours," I tell him, putting a flirty tone into my voice.

I watch him sit, feeling that excitable energy flood my system. The feeling that I always get when it's my time.

I'm no fool. I know exactly why this guy came over. And it wasn't for a seat.

He wants to fuck.

Meaning I get to have some fun tonight.

Angling my body toward his, I hold out my hand. "I'm Audrey," I tell him.

"Tate," he says. Taking my hand, he shakes it gently.

He thinks I'm delicate.

Idiot.

Letting go of his hand, I lean back in my seat and pick up my wine.

I cross one leg over the other, letting the skirt that Audrey dressed in this morning slip off my knee, revealing plenty of thigh.

His eyes drift to my legs.

So. Predictably. Easy.

I almost want to laugh.

Covering my smile with my glass, I take a slow sip of my wine before putting it back down.

I lean forward, place my elbow on the table, and rest my chin in my palm as I stare over at him. "So, tell me, Tate"—I let my teeth seductively graze over my lower lip—"do you live around here?"

Tate's eyes latch onto mine. His pupils dilate, and a slow smile spreads across his mouth.

He thinks he knows what I'm suggesting.

He has no clue.

No. Fucking. Clue.

Because men like Tate don't sense danger in attractiveness. They only think of one thing when they look at a woman like Audrey.

Sex.

They never see *me* coming.

And that works perfectly.

As I stand and leave the bar with Tate, his hand on my lower back, I smile inwardly, thinking to myself, *What an amusing irony it is that people like Tate are lured in by Audrey's beauty.*

Because, to me, there is nothing prettier than death.

And tonight … his death is going to look as pretty as hell.

ACKNOWLEDGMENTS

I'm going to keep this one short. But what I do want to say is that *Dead Pretty* has been my biggest challenge to date in my writing career. Amid a global pandemic, I wrote a book that tested me to my *absolute* limits, and I couldn't have done it without these handful of people.

My husband and children. There are no other three people in this world that I would want to be stuck in a house with for seven weeks and counting and continue to still be laughing and having the best time with. Infinity and beyond, my people.

Mostly, I owe the completion of this book actually happening to Vic and Tash. My Ungodly Hour Sprint Team. You both are my six-thirty-in-the-morning kick in the butt. I literally couldn't have finished this book without you both. And of course, I can't forget to mention Caaaaaaaaaaaarlllllllll!

My Wether Girls. My online home. To be surrounded by wonderful, supportive women such as you helps to restore my faith in the human race daily, and I've needed that reminder even more so these last few months.

Lastly, I would like to thank wine and coffee … my biggest supporters through all of this.

My P.S. thank-you, as always, is to you, those of you who are reading this right now. You sticking with me for all of these years and continuing to read the books that I put out are the reason I get to live and work my dream.

And lastly, a note: I know *Dead Pretty* is not the normal type of book you expect from me. I know it's probably a surprise. Maybe even a shock. I know because it shocked the hell out of me, too, that I could actually write a book like this! But I hope you enjoyed it. Maybe even loved it a little. And that it took your mind off the crazy world we're living in right now, if only for a short time. Stay safe. And until the next book …

OTHER BOOKS BY SAMANTHA TOWLE

STAND-ALONE NOVELS

CONTEMPORARY ROMANCE

Under Her

Sacking the Quarterback (BookShots Flames/James Patterson)

The Ending I Want

When I Was Yours

Trouble

ROMANTIC SUSPENSE

River Wild

Unsuitable

THE GODS SERIES

Ruin
Rush

SAMANTHA TOWLE

THE WARDROBE SERIES

Wardrobe Malfunction
Breaking Hollywood

THE REVVED SERIES

Revved
Revived

THE STORM SERIES

The Mighty Storm
Wethering the Storm
Taming the Storm
The Storm
Finding Storm

PARANORMAL ROMANCE NOVELS

The Bringer

THE ALEXANDRA JONES SERIES

First Bitten
Original Sin

ABOUT THE AUTHOR

Samantha Towle is a *New York Times*, *USA Today*, and *Wall Street Journal* best-selling author.

A native of Hull, she lives in East Yorkshire with her husband, their son and daughter, and three large fur babies.

She is the author of contemporary romances, The Storm Series, The Revved Series, The Wardrobe Series, The Gods Series, and stand-alones, *Trouble*, *When I Was Yours*, *The Ending I Want*, *Unsuitable*, *Under Her*, *River Wild*, and *Sacking the Quarterback*, which was written with James Patterson. She has also written paranormal romances, *The Bringer* and The Alexandra Jones Series. With over a million books sold, her titles have appeared in countless best-seller lists and are currently translated into ten languages.

Sign up for Samantha's newsletter
for news on upcoming books:
https://samanthatowle.co.uk/newsletter-sign-up

Join her reader group for daily man-candy pics,
exclusive teasers, and general fun:
www.facebook.com/groups/
1435904113345546

Like her author page to keep in the know:
www.facebook.com/samtowlewrites

Follow her on Amazon for new-release alerts:
https://amzn.to/2Y9zwSc

Follow her on Instagram for random pics and the
occasional photo of her:
www.instagram.com/samtowlewrites

Pinterest for her book boards:
www.pinterest.co.uk/samtowle

Also, Twitter to see the complete nonsense she posts:
https://twitter.com/samtowlewrites

And lastly, Bookbub, just because:
www.bookbub.com/authors/samantha-towle

Printed in Great Britain
by Amazon

26998045R00176